NH

Now...a
Harlequin
romance
by Anne Mather
comes to life
on the movie screen

starring

KEIR DULLEA · SUSAN PENHALIGON

Leopard in the Snow

Guest Stars
KENNETH MORE · BILLIE WHITELAW

featuring GORDON THOMSON as MICHAEL
and JEREMY KEMP as BOLT

Produced by JOHN QUESTED and CHRIS HARROP
Screenplay by ANNE MATHER and JILL HYEM
Directed by GERRY O'HARA
An Anglo-Canadian Co-Production

Other titles by
KATRINA BRITT
IN HARLEQUIN ROMANCES

Other titles by
KATRINA BRITT
IN HARLEQUIN PRESENTS

Many of these titles are available at your local bookseller
or through the Harlequin Reader Service.

For a free catalogue listing all available Harlequin Romances,
send your name and address to:

HARLEQUIN READER SERVICE,
M.P.O. Box 707, Niagara Falls, N.Y. 14302
Canadian address: Stratford, Ontario, Canada N5A 6W4

or use order coupon at back of books.

The Silver Tree

by

KATRINA BRITT

Harlequin Books

TORONTO • LONDON • NEW YORK • AMSTERDAM • SYDNEY

Original hardcover edition published in 1977
by Mills & Boon Limited

ISBN 0-373-02143-7

Harlequin edition published February 1978

PRINTED IN U.S.A.

CHAPTER ONE

Now that Diane was almost at the end of her journey a tiny spring of excitement welled up inside her. She was in Madeira at last, where one had to set the time back one hour. In the hurry and bustle of arrival Diane nearly forgot to alter her wristwatch. Everything had happened so quickly from leaving the ship to stepping in the hotel launch and being whisked ashore, there to be whisked up again in a lift to the hotel. As she left the lift her feet in soft white sandals had trodden a cobbled walk meandering in between exotic flowers of every hue to the white building set in immaculate lawns and date palms.

The interior of the hotel was cool, white and tranquil, with a uniformed porter to carry her case and lead her to her suite of rooms on the first floor. They consisted of a bedroom, bathroom, and lounge overlooking the sea, and Diane was drawn at once to the balcony to gaze out on the exquisite Bay of Funchal. With a breath of pure delight she gazed across the sunlit water and identified the three dark shapes away on the horizon as the Deserta islands. Then her eyes lowered on the gardens of the hotel where a wonderful range of flowers, shubs, and trees flourished with a tropical splendour which had to be seen to be believed.

The gardens dropped down in a series or terraces to water level and already the first flowers of spring were out in abundance. Waterfalls of bignonia Venusta, better known as golden rain, covered the slopes, along with hibiscus, scarlet poinsettias, gladioli, freesias, and begonias like cushions of pink snow. Diane lifted her face to the warm caress of the sun, letting it ripple luxuriously over her sun-starved limbs and, closing her eyes, breathed in the perfumed air tangy from the smell of the sea.

Somewhere on this tropical, steep volcanic island was the

pen-pal responsible for her being here. It had all started when Diane along with other girls at her school had begun to write to girls of their own age abroad. The headmistress of the girls' school she had attended had been all in favour of it since her pupils not only derived pleasure from it but it was also useful in an educational sense, since some of them learned quite a lot from countries they might never have the good fortune to visit.

Maria de Valmardi's letters had been written in beautiful copperplate handwriting on monogrammed paper, and at first Diane had been rather in awe of it. Then, as letters had been exchanged regularly, the monogrammed paper had been taken for granted, and they had continued to keep in touch after Diane had left school and gone to art classes. Now, at the age of twenty-one, Diane was a successful designer of fabrics and Maria was betrothed to a man of her parents' choice.

Maria was the youngest of three children. Alonso, aged twenty-eight, was the eldest, followed by Francine who was married with twin boys, and then Maria. Alonso, according to Maria, was very handsome and a bachelor. He led a full life and besides managing the estate filled his days with all kinds of sport. Until now he had managed to evade the matchmaking mammas by being seen occasionally in the company of the daughter of a distant cousin, Bella Vangroot. Reading between the lines, Diane felt that Maria did not fancy Bella as a sister-in-law, but she had thought no more about it until a rather disturbing letter had arrived several months ago from Maria. In it she had said that Alonso had seen the recent photograph which Diane had sent in exchange for one of Maria's at that young lady's request, and that he had fallen in love with her. The result was that Maria had enclosed travel tickets to Madeira for Diane to come to the Quinta de Valmardi. Diane must understand that Alonso could not send the tickets as it would not be right for a bachelor to invite a single young woman to his home unaccompanied.

Diane had been alternately shattered, then amused.

6

There had not been the slightest possibility of her accepting the invitation, of course, although she had felt the need to let Maria down lightly by promising to think it over. Since then the firm that had employed her had gone into liquidation and Diane had found herself at a loose end, with the travel tickets dangling before her nose like a tasty carrot. Why not accept Maria's invitation, one that had often been repeated throughout the years, just for the fun of it? Not that Diane could see herself falling in love so conveniently with someone who was already in love with her photograph. Decidedly not. She had her own ideas about falling in love with the one man who would fill her life, and neither money nor position entered into it.

In the end it was a particularly bad winter that drove her into accepting. Diane released the balcony rail and came back to the present, feeling the need of a cool shower. She was to be picked up the next morning to travel to the Quinta de Valmardi. From what she could gather Maria was away on a visit to her fiancé and Alonso was to pick her up on his return to the island after taking part in a yacht race.

Since the thought of Alonso filled her with apprehension, Diane put him firmly from her mind and revelled in a warm perfumed bath from which she emerged more relaxed and eager for her evening meal. The dress she slipped over her head was demure, simple and well cut in white. Her wardrobe had been chosen with the Quinta de Valmardi in mind, and the result was a few good class clothes that would always come up like new. Hence the chic little dress, which was accompanied by a gold chain padlocked bracelet.

A last critical look in her mirror before going to the dining room showed large clear hazel eyes between thick brown lashes gazing from a cream-skinned face and pink lips slightly parted to reveal small white even teeth. An ordinary face, Diane thought wryly, patting her copper-coloured hair and wishing nervously that she did not have to dine alone.

The dining room had a superb view over the bay and

Diane was glad that the smart waiter who came forward as she entered the room led her to a table for two by the window. He brought her an aperitif and she sipped it, looking out at the palms with their leaves bunched against the blue sky. Suddenly her heart lifted. It was a lovely place to be in, and she was going to see her friend Maria for the first time. Maria had become like a sister to her. As she had no family of her own since her aunt had died six months previously, Maria was important to her.

The tables around her were filling up rapidly and the sound of voices rippled across cut glass and silver as people began to eat and drink to the accompaniment of popping corks.

'Do you mind if I share your table?'

Diane looked up, startled, as the deep voice murmured above her ear, and the man went on apologetically, 'The other tables for two appear to be taken.'

A light-haired man of medium height was smiling down at her with blue twinkling eyes out of a rugged face. His features were pleasingly blunt with white teeth and his bulky shoulders reminded her of a baseball player even as his accent registered. An American, and definitely one of the sporty open-air type, Diane decided, and found her voice.

'Of course,' she said with a smile. 'Please sit down.'

His smile broke into a wide grin as he sat down. 'I hope I'm not intruding. Allow me to introduce myself—Dwight Rogan from Washington, returning from a yacht race which I did not win.'

He extended a large hand across the table. Diane blinked and found her own hand swallowed up in his paw. With her face the colour of a rose, she stammered, 'I'm—er—Diane McNair from the U.K., just arrived on a visit.'

He shook her hand firmly and took his time releasing it. 'Pleased to meet you,' he said soberly, surveying the slender hand looking fragile and pale against the tanned squareness of his own huge one. 'You have artistic fingers. My guess is that you're an artist of some kind?'

8

'You're right,' Diane laughed. 'I was a designer for fabrics until my firm went into liquidation a short time ago.'

'Was?' He raised a thick light brow. 'Does that mean you're on the market for a job?'

She nodded, and laughed at the concern on his face. It was a nice sound like a soft peal of bells, subdued like her voice. 'It's all right. I have some money saved.' With a feeling of embarrassment she added, 'Who won the yacht race?'

He shrugged, 'Someone from the island—the Duque de Valmardi.'

Diane's throat went dry. She stared, gulped and said weakly, 'Did—did you say—the Duque de Valmardi?'

'I did. You look kind of surprised. Do you know him?'

'No, I don't. What is he like?'

'Latin-looking. Young, very tall, very dark and a devilishly handsome son of a gun.' His blue eyes twinkled. 'The kind of man girls like you go dreamy-eyed about. You would approve of him. He's very gallant.'

Diane swallowed bleakly. 'I happen to be going to the Quinta de Valmardi tomorrow to visit Maria de Valmardi and her brother Alonso.'

He laughed at the consternation on her face. 'So what? Alonso might be a *duque*, but he's also a very nice guy.'

Diane gave him a grateful look. 'I'm awfully glad you told me about him—the Duque, I mean. You see, I had no idea they were so grand.'

She went on to tell him about Maria and their letters through the years. Instead of feeling that she was talking to a stranger, Diane felt that she had known her companion for years. He had that effect on her. He could not have been more than thirty, but in some way he seemed mature, a man of the world whom she could talk to and trust. But she said nothing about Maria sending the travel tickets or her reason for sending them. It had shaken her to realise that Alonso was a *duque*, and someone very important. He must be very wealthy to take part in yacht racing, and for the first time Diane began to have qualms about accepting Maria's invitation. The meal passed pleasantly despite her misgivings and she began to relax as the food and wine spread warmly inside her. Dwight, it appeared, had come to see friends on the island.

'I'm surprised you're not married,' he remarked during a lull in the conversation. 'What are the young men thinking about your way to let you remain single?' He grinned. 'But their loss is my gain. Not spoken for, by any chance, are you?'

His eyes were on her ringless hands and Diane shook her head. 'No, and I haven't come here in search of a husband, so you can forget my single state. What about you, since you're so much in favour of folks hitching up?'

He said ruefully, 'I'm always too busy to date anyone regularly. How would you like to come to the States?'

Diane smiled, liking his frankness. 'I'll think about it,' she promised, and delicately suppressed a yawn. 'Excuse me, but I'm feeling dreadfully sleepy. I suppose it's all the travelling and the change of air. It kind of bowls one over.'

He said mildly, 'I take it you're going to have an early night?'

She nodded. 'I want to be up early tomorrow to look around the town before I'm collected at eleven o'clock. It looks interesting.'

He nodded. 'It is. May I go with you? I would like to see the sun on that glorious copper hair of yours.'

Diane felt her face colour up. 'Thanks. I'll see you then,' she murmured. 'Excuse me, won't you?'

On the way to her room her steps were light and carefree. Dwight Rogan had been as good as a tonic to her after the shock of hearing that Maria's brother was a *duque*. The American's interest in her was flattering—not that it would go any further, however. She was here in Madeira at Maria's invitation and nothing else was important, not even the Duque's admiration of her portrait. A man in his position was not likely to lose his head over an ordinary girl like Diane McNair. The man could have been at a loose end between his various activities when he suggested that Maria should send her travel tickets to visit them. Also, he was

10

sure to be aware of the difference in their backgrounds socially. Even so, her visit promised to be more than a little intriguing, and Diane felt a bubble of excitement swell inside her. She could hardly wait for tomorrow when her visit would really begin.

The following morning Dwight was waiting for her in the dining room. He was wearing a lightweight suit in caramel gabardine and he looked her over appraisingly with a broad grin. The sun slanted in through the windows, coaxing her copper hair into flame, and his eyes lingered upon it as he drew out her chair.

'It's beautiful,' he said. 'You sure are a sight for sore eyes.' He dropped his gaze down over her youthful freshness, taking in the sun-suit in avocado green that reflected in the clearness of her lovely eyes, the long slim legs and sensible flat-heeled sandals. 'I'm glad you're not wearing high heels. The streets here are made of small stones forming mosaic patterns and they might look picturesque, but they're purgatory to walk on for long.'

Diane enjoyed her breakfast, for Dwight was a stimulating companion, but there was not much time for conversation if she had to be back at the hotel by eleven o'clock. She was also glad of Dwight's company to the town, for there was so much that was strange. The strong light, for instance, after the grey skies of England was startling. So were the strange smells from the shops mingling with the more appetising aromas from the restaurants.

They hired one of the oxen-drawn sledges into town. The padded seats were surprisingly comfortable and the pace was leisurely and cool. While Dwight bought presents for his friends, Diane shopped for herself and eventually lost him while looking for sandals with thick soles. As he had warned her, the stones lining the streets were very uncomfortable through thin ones.

The shops fascinated her and it was quite some time before she found what she wanted—a pair of soft leather, flat-heeled, thick-soled, sandals with an open heel. It was half past ten when they found each other and Dwight insisted on her going in a café for a cool drink and a rest before returning to the hotel.

It was obvious she was going to be late arriving back at the hotel and she hoped that the Duque would be delayed, thus giving her time to freshen up before meeting him. But as they approached the hotel her heart dropped to see a long black opulent car drawn up outside the entrance. Seated next to the driving seat was an extremely attractive young woman with a rather haughty face and gleaming black hair, who eyed her with interest.

'The Duque's car,' murmured Dwight above her ear. 'There he is coming out of the hotel. Goodbye. Have a nice time!'

Diane thanked him for being so kind and returned the pressure of his hand as he inserted his card between her fingers. Then her attention was no longer fully on him. Since his succinct description of the Duque de Valmardi, she was most curious. The sun dazzled on the entrance doors of the hotel as they swung open, and a man came striding out into the brilliant sunlight to pause and look around him.

Diane teetered and blinked. She had never seen such a devastatingly good-looking man in her life. Dwight had not exaggerated when he had said that he was attractive. He was tall, wide-shouldered, dark-haired, dark-eyed and vibrant. It was impossible for Diane to take her eyes off him as he looked around, presumably in search of herself. Then he was looking directly at her. The disturbing dark eyes between black lashes narrowed for a moment speculatively, and the next moment he was striding towards her with a smile that must have bowled more women over than any pop star.

No man had ever to her mind affected her so dramatically. Her legs did not appear to belong to her and her breath caught somewhere in her throat as she held out her hand.

'The Duque de Valmardi?' she said, pulling herself together firmly. 'I am Diane McNair.'

12

The dark eyes lingered for brief moments on her flushed face. Then he gave a slight bow. He spoke in excellent English.

'I recognised you from your photograph,' he said in a deep cultured voice that sent the blood coursing through her veins madly again. 'I must apologise for being late.'

Diane said politely in a low sweet voice, 'No apology is needed since I'm late myself. I've been shopping in the town.'

He glanced down at her purchases briefly and Diane tried in vain to stop the insistent pounding of her heart. Really, she told herself sternly, there was no need to get all strung up about a perfect stranger. At least he was not handing out the hot searching glances that the men in the town had done not many minutes ago. But he did make her feel, as they had, very conscious of herself as a woman.

He said politely, 'Do you want to put the parcels in your case, or would you prefer me to put them in the boot of the car?'

'Oh—er—in the car, I think, if you will. My case is already packed and waiting.'

Diane surrendered her purchases to his strong lean hands and faced the charm of that smile again. She wished she did not feel such an idiot, when he was so self-assured.

'Perhaps you will accompany me to the car and meet an old friend of the family,' he said.

She had forgotten the occupant of the car and turned her head to find that she was being observed very keenly from that direction. Some sixth sense told her that the woman observing her so keenly could be none other than Bella Vangroot, the daughter of a distant cousin of the Duque. She was right. The Duque introduced them smoothly, and Diane's smile was in marked contrast to the stilted acknowledgement of Bella, who languidly offered a black-gloved hand. Her dark eyes hovered for some time in the bright copper hair as if caught in its gleam before she nodded graciously.

The Duque had put her purchases in the boot of the car

and was now smiling from one to the other. Diane, conscious of her shiny nose and ruffled hair after a morning around the shops, wished fervently that she had the courage to insist on going to her room to freshen up before going on the journey. The Duque would, no doubt, have her case brought down to the car. Quite unconsciously she lifted a slim hand to pat her hair into neatness. The trouble was, it was naturally wavy and tended to look in disarray when it was not.

The action did not miss the Duque's eagle eye and he said smoothly with a hint of satire, bending his head to address the woman in the car, 'I suggest I take you home, Bella, while our young visitor freshens herself up after a tiring morning around the shops.' He straightened and gave Diane a look which made her dizzy. 'You will find me in the bar of the hotel. I have ordered lunch for us here.'

With a feeling that she had just had a reprieve from something dreadful Diane made her way up the stairs to her room. It was a puzzle to decide what troubled her the most. Alonso's charm? Bella's almost tangible hostility? Diane frowned. For someone who had been enamoured by her photograph, Alonso had been very, very cool in his greeting. He certainly was not the shy kind. Indeed, he gave her the impression that what he wanted he would set out to get in no uncertain manner. Those long tapering hands of his had been strong even in the brief impersonal grip of her fingers. It was a miracle, considering his undoubted charms, how he had managed to remain single for so long.

There was no doubt that he had everything a woman dreamed of in a man—good looks, charm, breeding and wealth, added to which he was no doddering old man. And if she, who was only mildly interested in men, found Alonso so devastating, how did Bella regard him? Besides, Bella was thirty if she was a day. Had she been waiting for the Duque? She must have had offers of marriage before the years had begun to creep on.

Diane was still making her mind up about them when

14

she went into the bar to meet Alonso. A slow flush infused her cheeks as she entered the room and Alonso moved his head to look directly at her. Taking long nonchalant strides, he came towards her.

'Would you prefer a drink before lunch?' he asked politely.

She shook her head and declined with thanks. 'I'm not much of a drinker,' she confessed, finding herself unexpectedly hypersensitive to the vibrant warmth of his masculine presence.

'Neither am I,' he answered. 'Shall we go in to lunch?'

In the flower-bedecked terrace of the dining room waiters were already serving lunch. Alonso seated her at a table for two in a corner overlooking the lovely Funchal bay, and ordered. For the main course they had tender steak in Madeira wine with mixed vegetables, during which Alonso asked if she had had a good journey and of her first impressions of Madeira. Feeling slightly in a dream, Diane answered his questions, wondering whether it was the wine or her giddy reaction to his nearness that was affecting her. When he suggested something called *barriga de freira* for dessert, a concoction of almonds beaten with eggs and sugar, Diane agreed, knowing that it would slide down her throat like the rest of the meal, delicious but tasteless.

She found herself wishing that Maria could have been there to ease the tension, though she was sure that it was all on her part. Alonso could not have been more charming and aloof. There was not the usual cosy tête-à-tête over coffee, though. True, Alonso sat back in his chair and inhaled from a cheroot which he seemed to enjoy, while surveying her flushed face between those incredibly long black lashes of his.

Diane did not smoke but accepted another cup of coffee to give her something to do with her restless hands. It was a new experience for her to be restless. Usually she was the most relaxed of people. Behaving naturally was part of her charm, for there was nothing false or evasive in her whole make-up. The frank open gaze from clear eyes was in no

15

way coquettish, and her smile, which was spontaneous, usually turned more than one man's head in passing.

The fascination that she had felt for him on sight still persisted, although he was so withdrawn. His spare, clean-cut look, that tantalising air of distinction clung around him like an aura that drew her like a magnet. She looked at him briefly, noted that the long cheroot was burning down and sipped her coffee slowly. In repose that well cut mouth suggested a trace of cruelty and one could well imagine those black eyes assuming an implacable firmness. He was a man who realised his position in society and acted accordingly. There would be no half measures where he was concerned, and it came to her suddenly why he had remained single for so long. Why else if not from an indomitable sense of resolve to have his own way in all things?

His car smelled of expensive leather, as he helped her in, slammed the door and strode around to the driving seat beside her.

Diane breathed in the scent of flowers and was putting it down to the perfume Bella had used, which now lingered in the back seat when Alonso reached out a long arm behind her and drew it back to present her with a bouquet of roses. They had apparently been waiting for her on the back seat of the car, hence the perfume.

'Welcome to Madeira,' he said.

'Oh, thank you! They're lovely.'

Diane buried her face in the dewy pink and red buds. They were smaller than English roses but they had a very sweet scent. Fleetingly she wondered if there was any special message with roses in Madeira and wished that she had learned more about the place and customs. But Alonso seemed to be preoccupied as he started the car off at speed. Soon they were travelling along the lovely Avenida do Infante with its plethora of picturesque white houses decorated by balconies, iron lanterns, imposing gates and brilliant flowering creepers.

There were bushes of beautiful pink, red, blue, yellow

16

and mauve flowers, amid scarlet poinsettias enhanced against a green ground, and the flowers were really breathtaking all the way to the sea. The banana groves, protected by windbreaks of bamboo, flashed by and still more grand villas this time in blue and white. They were cruising along the coast road now and Diane gazed out on people bathing with the majority sunbathing on gay mattresses.

'I trust you bought some warm clothes with you.'

Alonso's deep voice jerked Diane out of her reverie. He was turning the big car inland and roared up a steep road. Here the road widened and there were clear signs for the motorist of further zig-zag roads ahead.

Diane clung to the sides of her seat as Alonso swept the car expertly around hazardous bends and thought fleetingly of the soft angora dresses and alpine sweaters between tissue paper in her case. Then she tried to remember what Maria had told her about the geography of the island in her early letters.

'Maria did say that you were over a thousand feet above sea level,' she volunteered tentatively.

'One thousand eight hundred feet,' he said. 'And we are now in the residential part of Funchal. What exactly has Maria told you in her letters? Nothing very concrete, I will warrant.'

His dark eyes turned to slide over her flushed face looking as flower-like as the roses in her slender hands and he half-smiled.

'Maria told me quite a lot about the island and ...' Diane stopped and bit her lip, wondering if Maria had told her of her brother's admiration for her photograph with his permission. In any case, it would be polite for him to make the first move.

'Why have you stopped talking?' he demanded, swerving the car round a particularly hazardous bend.

Diane screwed up her courage, wishing he was less formidable. It could be her hypersensitive nature that had sensed a sudden withdrawal in his slow relaxed manner.

'I was only going to say that Maria had acquainted me

with a few facts about her family; that there were three of you, and that you and Maria are unmarried.'

Again the half-smile, and the well-cut lips were a little hard despite the smile.

A brief silence. Then he said coolly, 'I suppose you are aware that Maria's single blessedness will now be short-lived, since she is soon to be married.'

'I believe so.'

He drove for a while in silence. When he spoke again his eyes were kept gazing through the windscreen at the road ahead.

'You and Maria are of an age, are you not?'

'Yes. We are both twenty-one.'

'And have you broken as many hearts as Maria?'

Diane's hazel eyes opened to their fullest extent. 'If I have then I'm not aware of them. I'm not romantically involved with anyone, if that's what you mean.'

His voice had a hint of satire. 'You seem very quick to acquaint me of the fact that you are still single. I wonder why? Is it because you have no interest in men?'

'I didn't say that.' Diane's voice sharpened. For some reason she had the feeling that he was deliberately baiting her. 'One could say the same about you, that you aren't interested in women. After all, you're twenty-eight and unmarried.'

The moment the words were out Diane would have given anything to recall them. There was a long pause, then he said in a voice chipped with ice,

'That is my concern. How long do you intend to stay, Miss McNair?'

By now Diane was feeling somewhat bewildered. 'I haven't really thought about it,' she confessed helplessly. 'I'm between jobs at the moment.'

The car had stopped climbing and was now cruising along a tree-lined road with a distinct cooling of the air. It caressed Diane's flushed face and although her skin seemed to be burning her hands felt cold and clammy around the bouquet of roses. Did she imagine it, that she was not

18

exactly welcome? A swift glance at his clear-cut profile told her nothing.

'Indeed,' he observed calmly. 'May one enquire what kind of career you are engaged in?' Diane had an idea that he was frowning as he continued. 'I am afraid that I know little or nothing about you beyond the fact that Maria has continued corresponding with you through the years.'

'But you said that you recognised me from my photograph,' Diane insisted rather desperately.

She saw the dark silky brows uplift. 'That is true,' he admitted. 'Maria showed me the photograph in order that I should recognise you when you arrived. Incidentally, she was very upset at the thought of not being here to welcome you. I myself only just made it. No doubt Maria told you that I was taking part in a yacht race?'

Maria had, but Diane did not enlarge upon it. It was clear to her now that Maria had not been entirely honest concerning her brother in respect to herself. He had not been enamoured by her photograph, neither had he provided the travel tickets which Maria had sent to her. What was going on? At the moment she had not a clue, and it seemed that she had to wait to see Maria herself for some explanation. Meanwhile she had to endure the company of this autocrat of a brother. Pray heaven it would not be for long! With mixed feelings Diane noticed the magnificent views back across the harbour where a seaplane hovered, then they were turning into a drive between beautifully wrought iron gates which a man ran out to open for them. On they went, between magnificent tall trees and a sea of camellias. Diane had never seen so many of the lovely pink and white flowers, from young bushes to whole avenues of enormous trees of astonishing girth and age. She leaned forward eagerly in her seat to look at them in awe and she had to comment about them.

'How beautiful the camellias are!' she exclaimed, her clear eyes shining in admiration. 'The soil must be very fertile here.'

He flicked her a glance and slowed the car down for a woman to open the second pair of wrought iron gates. Her black garb and white buckskin shoes told Diane that she was a worker on the estate and she smiled as the woman bobbed a curtsey in reply to the Duque's uplifted hand.

He drove on and said, 'Madeira is about four hundred miles east of the coast of Morocco and is practically the same latitude as Casablanca. So it is not surprising that not only do we have fertile lime-free soil, which is responsible for the abundance of the camellias, but we also enjoy a temperate climate. Our summers rarely rise above eighty degrees and frost is non-existent, with winter temperatures varying between forty-five and sixty degrees.' The smile he gave her was slightly sardonic. 'You could say that it is a veritable Garden of Eden.'

But Diane was not listening. Her eyes were fixed on the *quinta* that they were now approaching. It was a mellowed stone building of old Portuguese architecture. Imposing towers joined a single-storied centre of tall windows forming an ideal ground floor section for gracious entertainment. In the mosaic-tiled courtyard orchids bloomed in large earthenware jars along with scarlet geraniums, giving an atmosphere of peace and gracious living. A manservant was there, wearing a white jacket over dark slacks, to take her case. His features were dark with black eyes that looked at her curiously before he obeyed the Duque's orders to take her case up to her room.

The housekeeper who came forward was very much like the manservant, with the same black eyes and courteous manner. 'Senhora Machini,' said the Duque. 'Our English visitor, Miss Diane McNair. The *senhora* will always have your welfare at heart while you are here, Miss McNair,' he finished courteously.

Diane offered a hand to the woman, who looked in her forties. 'I'm happy to meet you, *senhora*. I hope I do not give you much trouble.'

Through a hall with glimpses of beautiful old furniture gleaming in the muted light, Diane followed Senhora

Machini through a doorway and along a corridor to a further door and up a grand staircase in the centre of a hall. Following the woman's stiff black back, Diane spared a look at the many portraits lining the stairway and hoped mischievously that the rather long-nosed faces in their magnificent velvets and lace approved of her. She had arrived.

CHAPTER TWO

DIANE was dressing for dinner. After a shower in the dusky pink-tiled bathroom with thick soft fluffy pink towels on hand and a thick pile rug cosseting her bare feet warmly, she had returned to her bedroom to find that the maid who had unpacked her case earlier had laid fresh underwear out and one of her dresses, a silk jersey in a warm amber. Looking down at her dress, Diane decided that she was expected to dress for dinner at the Quinta but not too formally.

Sofia greeted her with a smile that put her instantly at her ease. Earlier on she had taken Diane on a short tour of the Quinta after bringing her a tray of refreshment. Like Sofia's English, Diane's Portuguese was limited, but she had discovered that smiles, nods of the head, and good manners worked wonders when the tongue failed to express.

'The *senhorita* has beautiful hair,' murmured Sofia gently, patting the springy waves into place after brushing the gleaming curls. 'It is like the sun when it rises in the morning, and will become even more beautiful after washing regularly in our fresh spring water.' She stepped away from the back of Diane to survey her handiwork, and gazed at their reflections in the mirror of the dressing table. 'Your skin, I think, needs little adornment. It has the delicate bloom of a freshly opened rose. I see many Englishwomen visitors and most of them cover their faces up with too much make-up. You have a natural look.'

The words were spoken sincerely and Diane got the gist of them.

'Thank you, Sofia,' she said. 'As I perspire more on my face and hands than I do on my body I naturally use make-up sparingly. As for my skin, one could say that the cold English weather is responsible for providing English-women with fresh complexions.'

Somehow they managed to make conversation, and if Sofia did not understand it all, her smiles and nods said that she understood most of it. Thanks to Sofia taking her around the Quinta, Diane was able to find the salon where she was to dine quite easily. She crossed the hall at the foot of the stairs and paused on the threshold of a beautifully proportioned room where chandeliers looked down softly on silk-panelled walls and a polished floor covered with expensive Chinese rugs.

Capacious settees and easy chairs upholstered in rich ruby velvet were placed about the room by the fireplace and the high windows which were adorned by matching fringed velvet drapes reaching to the floor. The furniture —tables, cabinets containing objets d'art, escritoires and buffets—had been created by superb craftsmen of long ago for gracious living. To her left an oval table in an alcove had been set for three people. Then the Duque was coming towards her, smiling urbanely, his teeth shining very white against the deep tan of his face.

His dark keen eyes flicked over her with no sign of expression in them. In that instance the room, to Diane, assumed a listening quality as he spoke.

'I trust you have rested, Miss McNair,' he said smoothly. 'Everything will, no doubt, appear to be very strange to you, including the Quinta itself. However——' His eyes seemed unwillingly to dwell upon her vivid face, making her nerves tingle, and she could not keep the swift rush of hot colour to her cheeks. 'We have only one guest for dinner.'

He escorted her to the fireplace where crackling logs burned cheerfully to keep the evening chill at bay and a subtle expensive perfume assailed her nostrils as she saw the Duque's cousin sitting on the settee flanking the fireplace. Her stiff charcoal grey taffeta gown with white lace trimmings looked regal and gave her a foreign air. The look in her dark eyes was more watchful than friendly.

Diane knew at once that here was one person who resented her presence at the Quinta and the Duque seemed to be making it two.

Her heart almost misgave her. There was something baffling, something one could even call sinister in his non-chalant movements as he poured her a drink and gave it to her as she sat down. The wine was comforting, to a certain extent warming her stomach and whetting her appetite. During the meal she expected awkwardness and constraint to reign supreme, but the Duque surprised her by his utterly relaxed manner and charm. She noticed that he treated Bella like a sweet sister, teasing her on occasions in a way which made her almost jocose. But she betrayed not the smallest desire to draw Diane into the conversation. It was left to the Duque to do that.

Her ideas of him became a whirl of conflicting emotions which utterly bemused her. Of one thing she was beginning to be surely convinced and that was that he was in some way responsible for Maria's absence from the Quinta. This was borne out by the rather strange looks in her direction from Bella, a searing intent gaze, then an instant falling of the full lids. It seemed as though they had joined forces together to form a bastion between their English guest and the Quinta.

Yet why should they do that? Diane asked herself this as they all adjourned to sit by the fireplace for coffee. A man-servant piled more logs on the fire as Diane took a chair opposite to Bella, who claimed her former place on the settee flanking the other side of the fireplace. The Duque took a stand at one corner of the fireplace to drink his coffee and to lead the conversation, which was mainly about the difference in the climate of Madeira and England.

'You had central heating, Miss McNair?' he enquired politely.

'Only in the flat I took when my aunt passed away not long ago,' Diane answered, feeling very de trop with a couple who lived, as it were, on another planet.

'You lived alone?' The black silky eyebrows rose more

than a fraction and Diane felt his disapproval as something tangible. But she had a feeling that her host would not find anything she did palatable.

'I did,' she corrected him quietly. 'I gave up the flat when my job ended in the liquidation of the firm.'

Bella put down her empty coffee cup carefully and fixed Diane's face with a rude stare. 'You surely did not expect to stay at the Quinta indefinitely?'

Diane had the feeling of being slowly drenched in very cold water as she met the dark eyes levelly. 'No, I did not. The fact that I happen to be between jobs doesn't mean that I have to cadge board and lodging. I am not entirely destitute. And now if you'll excuse me, I'm rather tired.'

She rose on shaking legs. For two pins she would go and pack her cases, refusing to stay even one night under the roof of this—this autocrat and the odious woman he was pleased to consort with. But before she reached the door the Duque was there before her with his long fingers curled around the door handle. Very quietly above her ear, he said, 'We will talk tomorrow. Do not forget that you are here at Maria's invitation. No one is ever rude to a guest at the Quinta. It will not happen again. Sleep well, Miss McNair.'

Diane was in bed when she heard the sound of the Duque's car revving up, then shooting away, taking with it the noise of the engine until it finally died away in the distance. He was, no doubt, taking his charming cousin, or whatever she was, home. What a woman, she thought, out to get her man. As for her quarry, Diane fell asleep telling herself that they deserved each other.

Amid the glory of exotic blooms with the air sweet with the scent of eucalyptus and pine, Diane ate her breakfast at the window of her room. The view took her breath away, the lovely bay of Funchal with the pretty roofs of white villas gleaming in the sun and the sweeping miles of beaches of warm pebbles washed by the frothy white breakers of a gentle sea. What a lovely place it was, she thought wistfully, knowing that she could have spent a wonderful holiday here under different circumstances.

The day promised to be warm and Diane thought longingly of the swimming pool at the back of the villa. During her tour of the Quinta with Sofia, there had only been time for a glimpse of it. Had Maria been home they would be splashing about in it like a couple of dolphins. According to Sofia, Maria's rooms were next door to those allotted to herself. It was comforting to know that Bella was not sleeping there. She was conjecturing about this when Sofia came to say that the Duque wished to see her.

Her first impression on seeing Alonso was that he had been in the swimming pool. He was all glow, sparkle and kinetic magnetism, a man of intense drive and energy which he controlled with the disciplined grace of an autocrat. She could imagine him doing a hundred push-ups in the morning as easily as any top-line athlete and he touched her emotions on a faint chill of pleasure overshadowed by doubt, a poised doubt but a serious one nevertheless. His damp hair was curling around his well-shaped head to lie in curly tendrils in the base of his strong neck, and his smile dazzled. Bareheaded, he was wearing cream slacks of impeccable cut with a white silk shirt and a dark red cravat tucked into the neck opening. He wore it casually with an air few men can command, making the simple attire interesting and correct.

He was waiting for her at the foot of the staircase, and as she joined him, he turned towards a door leading down a passage and out into the grounds.

He said evenly with the merest touch of his fingers on her elbow, 'We can take a walk in the grounds while we talk, but first I must apologise for the rudeness of my guest last evening.' He paused while he opened the door leading outside and allowed her to precede him into the warm caress of the sun. 'I am sorry, but it is easily explained since the *senhorita* has the interests of the Quinta at heart.'

'Naturally,' Diane returned dryly, ignoring the sharp look thrown her way from those dark keen eyes. 'When is Maria expected to return?'

'Soon,' he replied laconically, and they passed a giant tulip tree dwarfed by enormous conifers. Beyond these the garden began to drop into a series of terraces joined by steps and interspersed by fountains, statuary and pergolas of camellias and clematis.

The steps were broad enough for Alonso to walk by her side with his fingers around her elbow. Presently the gardens dissolved into woodland of glorious mimosa trees towering so high that Diane had to crane her neck to see the tops. By the side of the wood ran a long drive bordered by enormous old trees, and they strolled along this to branch off near the end of it on to a side path leading into the woodland.

Alonso said in a deep pleasing voice, 'An ancestor of mine, notorious for his love affairs, rode on horseback along this road with a maiden who had scorned his attentions and for whom he had fallen in love on sight. He carried her to the lodge we are now approaching in the woods and kept her there until her irate father came in search of her.'

'And that was the end of it?' Diane asked curiously.

'Indeed no. The girl refused to return home with her father because she had fallen in love with her captor. So although this ancestor of mine had indulged in many affairs, the girl he had abducted proved to be his last, for he married her and they had a family of which he was very proud.'

Wistfully, Diane said, 'She was very beautiful, of course?'

He shrugged wide shoulders with a foreign gesture. 'We are given to believe so by a diary which was found later and from paintings of her. But a woman's beauty lies in the eye of the beholder where a man in love is concerned. She had fiery hair and a temper to match, which was probably the reason her husband was faithful to her. He would not be

27

bored by a submissive wife, which she could never have been.

Diane said demurely, 'She must have had her moments of submission if she bore him a family.'

'That is so.' The dark eyes glinted momentarily and his mouth quirked. 'Have you ever been in love, Miss McNair?'

Wondering where the question was leading, Diane answered carefully.

'Like all girls of my age I've imagined myself in love heaps of times, but the feeling has usually fizzled out, sometimes before I've ever spoken to the man in question. Maybe I'm not the kind of girl to go overboard for any man.'

'But surely there is nothing more certain, since you have proved that you can fall in love,' he contradicted slowly, his eyes roving her heightened colour, before gazing at the halo around her copper-coloured head caught in the rays of the sun. 'You are of a sensitive nature. I have never seen anyone blush so readily. You ought to have been christened Rose, for your skin has the bloom of rose petals.'

For a moment Diane drowned in the dark eyes looking down at her so intently. His look unnerved her, sending vibrations through her body to her fingertips. More from embarrassment than anything, she said baldly, 'Thank you, but I'm sure you didn't bring me out here to tell me that.'

His smile was totally disarming and he lifted a brow. 'I can see I shall have to be on my toes where you are concerned. You are a little unexpected. However, I like your candour, but you have not been entirely honest with me, have you?'

Now it was Diane's turn to frown. 'I don't understand,' she answered stiffly. 'Define honest.'

'I asked you just now if you had any men friends, or words to that effect. You said no, and yet I distinctly remember Maria mentioning someone—a Max Delrose, a journalist friend of yours.'

Diane laughed, a sweet quiet sound which rippled over the air pleasantly.

'Oh, Max?' she exclaimed lightly. 'He's a distant cousin of mine and has made it his business to be responsible for me since my aunt died.'

'You have no other relatives? You are alone?'

'I have cousins abroad, but we never correspond.'

There was no time for further conversation and Diane was relieved. Her companion was far too discerning. He had confessed to knowing little or nothing about her, yet he appeared to know all the essentials. She could imagine him shooting a few economical questions at the naïve Maria and learning what he wanted without her being aware of it.

He was saying, 'This is the lodge.'

They were looking between the giant trees to a small clearing where a very substantial kind of hunting lodge loomed, remote and romantic. Diane tried to imagine the kidnapped maiden staring out from one of the windows and wondered if the Duque's ancestor was as handsome as he was. The man would probably be loaded with the Valmardi charm, which was why the girl had finally succumbed to him.

'Can we go inside?' she queried.

'Certainly. There is a key kept under the eaves.' Alonso strode forward and disappeared around the side of the building to reappear with a key which he inserted in the lock of the heavy front door. It opened easily and he stood aside for her to enter. Diane saw what she imagined was the main room, which was simply furnished with dark heavy furniture. A pile of logs lay in readiness by the fireplace and there were several genuine hunting prints on the walls.

Alonso explained, 'The winter mists bring a certain amount of damp, with the result that fungi grow rapidly, so fires are lighted at intervals to dry the place out. We used to play here as children and have raced many times along the tree-lined avenue on our way here. The last one to arrive always had to do the chores. All our vacations in the summer were spent here.'

Diane shone up at him, trying to envisage the three of them with the young Maria bringing up the rear. 'You would always be first, of course, with your long legs and extra years,' she said.

For several seconds the light which appeared suddenly in his eyes was tender and mocking. 'I always gave them a good start.'

Diane was beyond a mocking answer. Feeling very peculiar beneath that magnetic gaze, she gave her attention to the bookshelves each side of the huge stone fireplace. She would have loved to browse among them to see his favourite authors, but their visit was only brief.

They were walking back to the Quinta when she said, 'I had a very firm conviction when I was in the lodge that it had only known happiness. I would like to bet that the maiden your ancestor took there really enjoyed every moment of her captivity.'

'You could be right,' he agreed. He cast her a surprised look and sounded surprised. 'We all know that at the Quinta, but for you, a stranger, to feel the atmosphere of the place on so short a visit is truly remarkable.'

'Not really. Lots of people can sense an atmosphere in a dwelling.' Although Diane appeared on the surface to be normal her pulse had quickened, for the walk was now nearing its end and the purpose for which he had brought her outdoors was still obscure. Any moment now, she told herself, something either unpleasant or cataclysmic is going to happen. They had traversed the length of the tree-shaded avenue when he said, 'You and my sister Maria have corresponded for some years and during that time you have learned much about her?'

'I suppose so.'

'You know, of course, that owing to her sheltered life, she is very young at heart and a little naïve?'

'I know that Maria is a sweet and lovely person. I was very happy to hear that she's going to be married.'

'You were? You did not try to influence her in any way about it?' he asked sardonically.

'Why on earth should I?' Diane exclaimed resentfully. There was something in his tone that made her bridle, almost a note of censure.

'Then perhaps you did it unknowingly.' He said no more but helped her up the terraces with a hand on her elbow rather quickly so that she was breathless when they reached the lawns of the Quinta.

'Shall we sit down? We must have this talk before Maria returns.' His voice was light enough, but Diane felt a thread of iron beneath it. 'I will tell you my view of what seems to me to be a very strange situation. Shall we sit under the silver tree?'

He guided her to a beautiful silver tree beneath which was a garden seat. Like the rest of the trees in the garden it was massive and truly breathtaking. Diane sat down in one corner of the seat, and Alonso, hitching up immaculate slacks, dropped into the opposite corner to face her, his arm along the back of the seat.

He said, 'Maria has had a surfeit of admirers, many of which we did not approve. One in particular, a certain Pedro whom she met under romantic circumstances, was totally unsuited to her in every way and caused us much concern. We had always taken it for granted that she would eventually marry a very suitable young man who not only grew up with us, but who has loved her for a long time. But no, Maria was against it, and do you know why?' He fixed her coldly with his dark eyes. 'She wanted to be like you, and choose her own husband. Your English customs and ours are very different, and I am confident that if Maria had not corresponded with you through the years, she would have settled for Felipe Moltardo.'

Diane, stung by his whole manner, said indignantly, 'I can't accept it as being my fault. I have never tried to influence your sister in any way. My letters to her have contained nothing more than the usual news of my girlish activities in exchange for hers. I'm not a very gregarious type of person and all my outpourings have been the usual day-to-day accounts of a well brought up person.'

He inclined his head and said coolly, objectively, 'I appreciate that, but your kind of freedom as a young unattached woman is far different from Maria's. The Portuguese are inclined to protect their young offspring from the pitfalls which beset them in adolescence.'

Diane cut in at this point hotly and indignantly, 'And so are we. We have more freedom because our educational system perhaps has tended to become more enlightened than yours.' She blushed at his lifted brows and longed to slap him. How dare he sit there like a Daniel in judgement?

Sardonically, he replied, 'I could say a lot about that—but we are forgetting what this conversation is all about. To continue. When Maria invited you to the Quinta I regarded it as a gesture which would bring you here as her ally—in short, to help her in her stand for independence and in her refusal to marry Felipe.'

'You mean the invitation came solely from Maria without the approval of your mother or yourself?'

He lifted wide shoulders. 'We gave our approval for two reasons. One because Maria is very fond of you and lays great store by what you say and do. The other because we hoped to get you on our side.'

Diane stared at the lean brown handsome face, the clearcut aristocratic nose and firm determined jaw. She could see what Maria was up against. It probably was not Maria's mother who was insisting upon the match but Alonso himself. As head of the family since his father was deceased, he was laying down the law in his own right. But what shook her more was the fact that he had not fallen in love with her photograph. Indeed, right now there was veiled hostility in his eyes as if it would give him the greatest of pleasure to sweep her up in those strong arms and carrying her to the beach, toss her into the sea.

Her voice, when she could command it, was low, controlled. 'You are asking me to do the very thing which you have just accused me of. I would not dream of doing any such thing. I want no part of it. Maria must choose for herself. It is her life and neither I nor you have a right to interfere in it.'

Alonso's dark intense eyes narrowed and his nostrils thinned. It was obvious that he was controlling his anger in the courteous way to which he was accustomed.

'I accept your decision, of course,' he conceded coldly. 'But only on the understanding that I will not brook any interference on your part to influence Maria in this matter. I also trust that our conversation will go no further than this garden seat.'

'I don't usually betray confidences. What Maria has told me in her letters is known to no one but myself As for being invited here to the Quinta, I ...' Here her voice faltered, for never had she felt so alone, so utterly disappointed in what she had expected. But no matter, she would leave as soon as she was packed She lifted her chin and looked him in the face. 'I will leave immediately. Far be it from me to upset you and your household. Please excuse me—I'll go and pack.'

Diane was on her feet, her hazel eyes bright with the threat of tears. All the pleasure she had enjoyed through the years from writing and receiving letters from Maria was swept away as though it had never happened by this lean autocrat who behaved like God in his own household. In that moment she hated him and all he stood for. But she was not to escape so easily, for his hand shot out and her wrist was taken in strong fingers.

'Sit down,' he commanded. 'I have not finished.'

'But I have Please release my wrist. You're hurting me.'

'You have only to sit down and your wrist will be freed.'

By now Diane was past arguing. A few words and she would burst into tears and shame herself before this implacable man. There was a brittle silence and her wrist was released as she sat down. She felt uncomfortable at his nearness, a feeling of unease that had begun when his strong fingers had closed around her wrist. She could not understand it. Her head was beginning to ache and she wondered what she had let herself in for.

It was obvious that the Duque was not in favour of the English way of life. His tone of voice had clearly indicated this. What was more, some of that dislike had been directed at herself unless she was mistaken, and he was the kind of man who had no time for women. He was looking at her directly and there was a faint gleam in his eyes.

'I must apologise for seizing your wrist,' he said. 'However, it was the only way of stopping you. Servants are notorious gossips and we have never yet treated a guest discourteously at the Quinta. As for you leaving, it is out of the question, since Maria will be brokenhearted to find you gone when she arrives home. I am much too fond of my little sister to cause her any distress that is unnecessary.'

Diane's fingers had moved unconsciously to her bruised wrist. 'And any distress you might cause her by insisting that she marries this Felipe is necessary?'

'It is necessary for her happiness. Believe me, I know she loves Felipe and if we had forbidden her to have anything to do with him she would have married him like a shot.'

Diane appreciated the import of his words, but it did not endear her towards him. He was far too much man, even more so than the ancestor of his who had carried the maiden off to the lodge in the woods. It was not hard to imagine him doing the same thing with her to keep her silent if she did not agree with him. Would she end up loving him if he did? One thing was certain—life at the Quinta could become very complicated if she did not take care. The Duque was, and there was no doubt about it, a dangerous man to cross swords with—dangerous indeed—but devastingly so.

'You will like my mother,' he went on. 'She is an American from Boston. Everyone loves her here at the Quinta and she simply adores Maria. The beauty of the gardens here owes much to her. This silver tree she brought from Table Mountain, and there are countless trees and shrubs that owe their existence to her here in the gardens. While a superb climate and fertile soil do much to make a garden the care and love of gentle fingers is the magic which makes it exceptional and beautiful.'

He went on to point out a particularly beautiful pink campanula shrub brought from the Azores with drooping waxy bell-shaped flowers of deep pink which, he said, framed a breathtaking canopy in the summer. Diane found herself listening to his deep voice as he explained about the varied and interesting flora of Madeira set among African lilies and South African proteas. The latter, like a giant everlasting flower, ranged in colour from pale green to .cream, yellow, pink, mauve and red with black tips.

Diane was thinking how cleverly he had changed the subject when a footman appeared to say that the Senhorita McNair was wanted on the telephone, a certain Senhor Rogan.

'Dwight Rogan the yachtsman?' Alonso asked with uplifted brows.

Diane nodded. 'Yes. We met at the hotel in Funchal. Excuse me.'

She ran into the Quinta on light feet. Bless Dwight Rogan, she thought, for giving her a feeling that she had a friend on the island. One had to have someone as an ally against the Duque de Valmardi.

'Hello,' she cried as she picked up the telephone. 'How nice of you to call me!'

'Nice to hear your voice,' was the reply. 'Will you dine with me this evening? I'm staying with friends about twenty minutes' drive from your Quinta.'

Diane hesitated, wondering if it would be politic to accept his invitation so soon after her arrival at the Quinta. On the other hand it might save her an embarrassing tête-à-tête with the Duque that evening. He had said Maria was returning soon, but surely not that day?

'What's cooking? Has the Duque got you in a clinch?' Dwight's voice was filled with laughter.

It echoed in Diane's slim throat and lingered pleasantly on the air.

'No, of course not. You see, I don't know what has been arranged for this evening,' she replied, and turned as if some sixth sense told her she was being watched.

Alonso stood in the doorway behind her and she addressed him across the expanse of tiled floor.

'Mr Rogan wants me to dine with him this evening. He's staying with friends not far from here.'

Alonso strolled slowly across the hall towards her and said with a hint of satire, 'The man does not believe in letting the grass grow under his feet. Do you want to go?'

He paused a few feet away and looked down at her. The dark eyes met her own quizzically, and Diane felt her face go hot beneath his scrutiny. Drat the man! she thought irritably. If only one could know what he was thinking. He was so cool, so self-possessed. One felt it instinctively in the careless ease of his stance.

She drew a deep breath and her answer came jerkily as if she needed more breath to complete a whole smooth reply. 'I was thinking about what you have arranged for this evening. Will it be convenient for me to accept?'

He flicked a glance at her tentative smile and his eyes narrowed down to her slender figure.

'Why not ask your friend here for the evening?' he suggested crisply.

'Oh! Shall I?' Her eyes widened and she smiled at him. 'Thank you.'

Dwight accepted the invitation and agreed to come at eight o'clock as the Duque suggested. When Diane put down the telephone he was still standing there.

'I need hardly remind you,' he said. 'that what we talked about earlier is confidential. I do not want Maria to know, or anyone outside the family. Her whole future depends on the outcome of your visit to us, which I hope,' here his eyes twinkled down at her disconcertingly, 'you will enjoy. You are free to come and go as you choose.'

Diane felt her hackles rise at the way he took it for granted that she was staying. 'I don't think I said that I was staying, did I?'

His wry smile seemed to be saying that it was a foregone conclusion since he knew her fondness for Maria. 'In that case, I suggest we go into Funchal for lunch and I can show you something of our ways and customs.' He consulted his wrist watch. 'Shall we say in half an hour?'

Diane was ready in five minutes, dressed in cream sleeveless crisp cotton edged with navy and a cool little biscuit straw hat on her copper hair. As if on cue Alonso met her in the hall, flicked an appraising glance over her youthful sophisticated slimness and led her out in the strong sunshine to his car. He had changed into a lightweight summer suit and he looked elegant and completely at his ease as he set the car in motion with his lean strong hands.

They had left the Quinta far behind when he spoke. 'Do you like this Dwight Rogan?' he asked casually.

Diane was gazing out wide-eyed at orange and yellow speckled orchids growing in profusion like potatoes and beautiful woods of feathery mimosa.

'He's the kind of man one can't help liking,' she confessed. 'Do you know him?'

'I know of him. His father is Dwight Rogan senior, a millionaire in real estate. My mother knows him well.' A pause, then, 'You like Americans?'

'I like all kinds of people.'

'Do you think that money and position are essential in marriage, Miss McNair?'

Diane laughed. It was a pretty tinkling sound which made him turn his head to give her a more than interested glance. He met frank clear eyes between a thick fringe of eyelashes and fresh pink lips parting to show neat white small teeth.

'In other words, would I marry for them?' she mocked. 'I couldn't say. I've never been tempted. I must confess, though, that I expect to fall in love and marry in that order be he a beggar or a king.'

His voice was equally mocking. 'You are a romantic.'

'Yes, I am. Every true woman is. It's the eternal feminine trait in her. Some men are too, only many of them won't admit it. They regard it as a sign of weakness. That's why I admire that ancestor of yours who abducted the lady of his heart.'

He twisted the car round a bend and Diane found herself gazing out on silvery green sugar cane and banana plantations with the terra-cotta roofs of white and yellow cottages a flicker of flame in the greenery.

'So you are a romantic. No doubt you have told Maria that some day some gallant knight on a white charger will come along and carry her off to his castle.'

Just faintly, Diane stiffened. 'No, I have not told Maria any such thing. Maria is quite capable of her own dreams. If anyone is to blame for her being romantic then it's you, Senhor Duque, for keeping her in an ivory tower instead of letting her have more freedom.'

'That is a very fine English opinion, Miss McNair. Fortunately we live in Portuguese fashion and perfer it that way. We believe in following the traditions and cultures that have made our country great.' He also had stiffened somewhat and the dark glance was reflective. 'Did you see much of Funchal during your short sojourn there?'

Diane blinked at his adroit switching of the conversation, but let it pass. The man was obviously monarch of all he surveyed and was telling her politely that he would brook no interference in that quarter.

'I went round the shops,' she answered evenly. 'There wasn't much time for sightseeing.'

As they neared the town the air pulsated with warmth. Wherever Diane looked, away from sparkling sea, where dim islands were smudges through the haze, falls of bougainvillaea cascaded over garden walls and banana groves in glowing magenta, intense and brilliant. It was repeated in crimson, orange and deep pink into the town, startling the eyes with its colour. Dried river beds meandering through avenues into the town were flanked with it on either side, giving the impression of rivers of flowers.

They passed public gardens dense with trees and foliage in Funchal's main avenue and Diane saw shoeshine boys in their stand beneath the palms plying their trade. Country people were wending their way to and from the market with a leisurely gait. The men were broad and stocky with well worn shirts and wide-bottomed trousers, much washed and patched. Their trilby hats had flat crowns in traditional Portuguese style.

The women mostly wore black, black shawls and black full skirts, and over their black hair fastened at the back were the black squares they favoured. But if the colour was drab and more like a uniform, the women's faces were not.

They had a kind of gypsy look about them which reminded one of the passionate Moors. Something primitive, even fiery, seemed to lurk behind their black eloquent eyes. Some of them carried baskets on their heads balanced on a folded shawl to take the weight. All their movements were beautiful, sensuous and graceful. They walked straight backed with a becoming dignity, and Diane loved the saucer-eyed youngsters, especially the girls with their shy white smiles and the glint of gold rings in their pierced ears.

It had been downhill all the way into the town with breathtaking views from the hills of the sea and land. Diane had thought that the Governor's palace looked like a Moorish fort, but the ducks sailing in a pond around the white statue of two small boys had made her smile as they had entered the town.

The streets were bustling with activity when Alonso parked the car and took her into the fifteenth-century cathedral to see the architecture. From there they went to a wine lodge which one entered through a courtyard of cobblestones with hanging flowers and plants giving it a cheerful air. They passed through the bottling department where first the bottles were washed out with Madeira wine and the corks as well. Then they were filled automatically and corked later, passing on to a cork trimmer before being plunged into clean water and placed on to a drying tray.

In another room barrels were being prepared and used casks were being washed by the method of pebbles and fresh water. Diane gazed on enormous vats of wine which, Alonso said, took up to sixty years to mature. He went on to say that the buildings had originally been an old convent, hence the beautiful wooden floors, high-ceilinged rooms and magnificent teak-beamed arches and pillars.

At a teak barrel table with frescoes around the walls showing the vineyards they sampled the wine. Diane tasted Sercial, a dry wine, and Boal Solera, a sweet one, but found the

Malmsey and Terrantez more to her liking. Alonso watched her sample them with mocking amusement, especially when her eyes widened at the skull caps to which two long pigtails were attached worn by the waiters.

Diane, suddenly aware of Alonso's scrutiny, tried to play it cool, but the warm feeling inside her, which she felt was not entirely owing to the wine, was accentuated when he lightly clasped her elbow again on their way out. It would be so easy to fall for his undoubted charm, she thought, and wondered how many women had already done so. She had tried her best to unwind in his company, had even asked intelligent questions during their tour of the wine-making which he had answered equably. But he had remained his usual enigmatic self.

He did not take her through the bustling markets, but he did buy her a bouquet of flowers from the women flower-sellers in their red native costumes. Diane accepted the camellias, roses, violets and fern with a deepening of her colour as she thanked him.

'You are fond of flowers?' he asked on an uplifted brow. 'You should be very happy here in Madeira, for that is one thing we have a surfeit of.' He lifted a strong brown wrist and consulted his watch. 'It is lunch time. We had better make tracks for something to eat.'

'What else do you like?' Alonso queried carelessly as he swept the car up an incline, passing stalls shining golden with tangerines, pumpkins, custard apples, pineapples and passion fruit.

Diane gave this a few seconds' thought, then, 'I love the spring and the summer, the lovely changing colours of autumn, long walks over the downs with the summer rain on my face or walking in tangy frosty air.'

'You will not experience any walks here in frosty air, but you will derive the same amount of pleasure from walking in the hills where the air is tangy from the sea and fresh even in summer. As for the rain, we have our share and it can look as grey here as it does in London. You think you will enjoy your visit?'

Again a small pause, during which he shot her a curious look. Diane smiled.

'You sound like a travel agent coaxing me to like the island,' she said, and then wished she had not said it. No man, especially a *duque* would be at all flattered to be likened to a travel agent. Alonso was no exception.

He said stiffly, 'While Madeira depends a great deal on tourism it is in no way to be compared with your English holiday resorts. It does not close down any of the amenities during the off season. Everything goes on just the same. The change is a subtle one, a pleasant peaceful atmosphere which pervades the whole island, though Funchal is the main target for holidaymakers. We do not hibernate, of course—I mean that Funchal never falls into an idle limbo.'

Diane stole a glance at his clear-cut profile as he spoke. His appearance, everything he represented was coloured by the bloom of perfection which when viewed by present-day standards was nothing short of miraculous. Of course, he was an exception, for there was an aura about him that was strictly personal. What kind of chemistry went into producing such a man, Diane had not a clue. Neither had she to the reason why he should colour her day even to the point of miraculous felicity in a way that she did not want it to end.

She recalled her surprise on seeing him for the first time outside the hotel in Funchal, and the way her whole being had quivered into new life. Now since he had presented her with the flowers, for some idiotic reason, she felt shy of meeting his eyes. They had left the town behind and were speeding along the coast road. The air was soft and warm and filled with a golden, clearly translucent light which is one of the lovely features of a fertile land which experiences the essential benison of rain.

Eventually Alonso ran the car off the road into the court-yard of a small tavern. The dining room they entered was a long, whitewashed, teak-raftered room. Their table for two by the window had evidently been reserved, for an older member of the staff came forward to greet them courteously.

41

It was the proprietor himself who came to take the Senhor Duque's order, attended by two waiters.

Delectable fish soup was followed by whiting with egg sauce, salad with a delicious dressing, fresh fruit including cherries and figs, Madeira wine and coffee. They lingered over their coffee laced with brandy while the daughter of the house strummed a guitar and sang a *fado*, a folk ballad. It was very sad, all about a girl whose lover had deserted her. Alonso interpreted it to Diane under cover of the applause with a mocking glint in his eyes.

The rest of the day went like a breeze. After lunch they went to see the basket weaving and another industry for which the island was most famous, embroidery. It was begun by an Englishwoman, a Miss Phelps, in the year 1856 and had spread to employ thousands of women and girls throughout the island. Alonso said that she would see many of them working in groups outside their cottages around the island. Diane digested this in silence and could not resist saying, 'Good for Miss Phelps. I take it you entirely approve of her influence here?'

He turned his head to look down at her with a dazzling smile. It was so unexpected with his dark eyes, so white against the tan of his face as his teeth gleamed, that Diane smiled back spontaneously.

'I approve,' he said, resting his disturbing glance on her copper-coloured head. 'Miss Phelps left a beautiful memory behind her which colours many lives.'

And shall I? Diane thought. Shall I leave memories for this arrogant *duque* when I've gone? I doubt it.

On the way back to the Quinta they ran into a shower of rain. Alonso set the windscreen wiper going and tossed her a sardonic grin.

'Are you still determined to go even when we have put on a shower of rain to make you feel at home?'

She managed a fairly prompt reply. 'I want very much to see Maria, who has seemed like a sister to me through the years, a sister I've never had. After that, who knows?'

She shrugged slim shoulders, determined not to let him

see that she was frightened by him in any way. She was finding Madeira as unexpected as he was, smiling at her one moment with the charm that would penetrate the hide of an elephant, then looking down that long aristocratic nose of his as if he thoroughly disapproved of her. Well, she could disapprove of him too, but she would find it infinitely harder to forget him than he would to forget her.

CHAPTER THREE

DIANE was about to dress for dinner that evening when Sofia came dark, brown and smiling with the clothes she had collected from Diane that morning to be washed. They glowed with an arresting brightness and freshness, having been laundered to a delicate perfection. Diane was delighted and thanked her warmly, complimenting her on how beautifully they had been done, and Sofia, pleased that she had brought pleasure to the English Miss, helped her to dress happily. She chatted in simple Portuguese with Diane learning, nodding and making deprecating gestures in between. At times they giggled helplessly over misunderstandings, leaving Diane smiling long after Sofia had left the room.

She leaned out from her balcony window to see that the rain had stopped, leaving the air filled with the scent of rich, newly washed earth. There was little or no twilight and the swift darkness threw mysterious shadows across the garden where diamond drops of rain glistened on the wisteria and bougainvillaea beneath her window.

Out in the bay a ship lay at anchor silhouetted sharply against a mellow darkening sky and lights were beginning to dance on the water. One by one lights were appearing in the villas on the mountainsides and Diane could imagine them lighting up the cobbled streets in the town, reminding one of a place indifferent to change. When an arc of car lights swept the garden, she turned from the window, knowing that Dwight Rogan had arrived. The thought of his broad smile and rugged friendly face was reassuring as she made her way downstairs.

To her surprise there was a small gathering of guests when she entered the *sala*. The Duque, it seemed, had kept the number even, eight in all which included Dwight Rogan and the couple with whom he was staying. They were the first guests Diane met on entering the room. Dwight introduced his host and hostess as Gwen and Cyril Taylor, Americans who had settled in Madeira some years ago. Then the Duque was there, taking Diane away to introduce her to his other guests. They were two well dressed couples with Portuguese names which Diane knew she would never remember. Neither were very young and could have been in their forties, but they were pleasant and courteous, and obviously very interested in the English Miss who had written to Maria for so long.

Dinner proved interesting through the many and varied courses with silent waiters flitting around like shadows seeing that no one was left with an empty glass or plate. And, as Diane had expected, Alonso was the perfect host, witty brilliant in repartee and revealing a congenital sense of humour. The small number of guests to him were easy to entertain for, no doubt, he would be used to more lavish entertainment. Diane, glancing along the table at his twinkling dark eyes and arresting dark handsome features, told herself that he had gone up one in her estimation by not inviting the odious Bella to dinner. Maybe, she thought, he was punishing her for being so rude to his English guest that first evening. But she doubted this. The more practical reason for that lady's non-appearance would be because of a previous engagement.

The meal was made more enjoyable for Diane because everyone spoke English, including Alonso's Portuguese friends, who spoke it faultlessly. Could that be the reason the Duque had invited them? To put her at her ease? To persuade her to stay? Diane did not honestly think so.

On the whole it was not a bad evening for Diane, who would have liked to have had the chance to talk to Dwight who sat opposite her at the table. She sat between one of the Portuguese couples who naturally compared their way of life to her own. Later they all sat around a low table in easy chairs for coffee and were entertained by two young singers, a boy and a girl who sang *fados* both sad and gay accompanied by a guitar.

During the evening Dwight asked her to go with him to Monte for the famous toboggan run over the cobblestones the next day and the Taylors, with whom he was staying, insisted on them going to dinner the following evening after their day out. To Diane it sounded fun, which she badly needed at the moment, and she accepted. Dwight was to collect her the following morning at ten, and the thought gave colour to her evening as the last guests departed.

Diane strolled out with Dwight to his car and when he had gone she lingered in the scented darkness. How enjoyable and leisurely the evening had been, she thought, with none of the usual frenzied changing back home when dining out. There was often a breathless arrival at the party with most of one's surplus energy burned out before the evening began. Now, when the evening was spent, one could stand and look out over the darkened bay, breathe in the perfume of flowers borne gently on the soft breeze rustling the palm trees gently in their sleep. She was going to miss all this beauty which caught at the heart strings when she went home.

'Is there anything more beautiful than the exquisite loveliness of a Madeira night?' Alonso whispered above her ear.

Diane started slightly, instantly aware of the masculine fragrance of a cheroot that he was smoking. He was very close and Diane felt her heart leap strangely.

'Yes,' she managed on a breathless note. 'I was just thinking the same. There's a wonderful sense of stillness and a peace in which one can relax naturally and enjoy all the sleeping beauty around one.' She drew a deep breath. 'There are so many different scents. I can smell eucalyptus.'

'Come, I will take you to the tree. We had better keep to the path—the grass will be soaked from the recent rain.' He led her along a paved path across the lawns to an enormous tree and reached up a long arm to take off one of

46

the leaves. 'Crush it between your fingers and smell it,' he said, giving it to her.

Diane did so and put it to her nose. The smell of eucalyptus was very strong, and she laughed as if making an exciting discovery. 'It's far different from the kind one buys from the chemist, kind of more oily and fresh,' she said.

The moon coming up slowly lighted up her glowing face and shining eyes.

His glance slid over it and he said, 'The real thing is always better than the substitute.' He dropped the butt of his cheroot and ground it out with his heel. 'A word of warning about the sun,' he continued. 'While it possesses neither gentleness nor humidity you will discover that it is not enervating nor too hot. But do not allow this to disarm you as to its power. It is important for you to become acquainted with it by degrees, say about fifteen minutes or so on the first day, increasing the time as you go on. Otherwise you will suffer intense discomfort and pain. Usually it only takes a week for one to become acclimatised.' He paused and again that rapier-sharp glance took in her delicate profile looking pale and ethereal in the moonlight. 'I would say that your skin is not tough, so I would advise caution.'

'Thank you,' she said, gazing out at the ridge of mountains to her left sprinkled with lights glittering like jewels in the scented darkness. The eucalyptus leaf in her hand was forgotten as she savoured moments in life that would always be remembered. Silence fell between them, silence which Diane knew her companion shared as he looked out over the bay turned silver in the moonlight. How long they stood she never knew, but she had the strangest feeling of being on the same wavelength as the tall, dark, enigmatic man at her side. Whether it was the magic of the night air playing tricks she was never sure, but the feeling was there so strong that it was left to him to break the silence.

'Shall we go in?' he said. 'You have had a long day. Come.'

They had entered the Quinta and Diane was about to leave him to go to her room when he said, 'I shall be away for most of tomorrow. I believe the American is calling to take you to Monte. Take care.'

Diane was in her room before she began to think about his warning. What did he mean, take care on the toboggan run or take care with Dwight? But it was not actually his words that remained with her until she slept, it was his dark eyes meeting her own in a deep penetrating look. There were depths in him that no one was allowed to reach, least of all Diane McNair. It was on this disturbing thought that she went to sleep.

Diane was up early for breakfast in her room—eggs, fresh warmly crisp rolls with fresh Madeira butter, a large dish of fruit and lots of hot coffee. The Duque had left the Quinta before she was up. The sound of his car leaving had awakened her For a while she had lain in bed watching the sun spread stiff fingers of light across the room and had welcomed the warmth of a new day seeping into her body Then she had remembered that Dwight Rogan was calling for her at ten o'clock and had left her bed, hastily putting on a wrap.

No one met her on the way downstairs through the elegant corridors and past rooms where grandiose arrangements of flowers were arranged fresh each morning in extravagant vases in the corridors. The bouquet of flowers the Duque had given her the day before had been arranged beautifully in her room and there would be others to keep it company later. In the garden with its miraculous view of the sea and the bay shimmering beneath a blue sky, Diane walked between the masses of flowers in their pinks, blues, purples, golds, velvet magnolia, and passionate reds.

She paused to breathe in the different scents and her eyes strayed across the lawn to the vast eucalyptus tree. Then she took a path in the opposite direction, down a cobbled path and peeped around a wall of poinsettia, plumbago and bougainvillaea to look longingly at the swimming pool. The blue water looked inviting, but she could hardly use it without permission. If only Maria would come home! There would be heaps of time to swim in the pool with her then. Diane closed her eyes and thought of swimming in that beautiful water, basking on the side on one of the loungers. then swimming again. Heavenly thought! ·

Slowly she retraced her steps, to cannon into one of the gardeners who came around the wall of plumbago.

Respectfully making a small bow, he said, 'Bom dia, minha menina.'

Diane answered in Portuguese and gave the man a warm smile before going quickly into the Quinta. The poor dear had looked quite startled, she thought impishly—and no wonder He had probably never seen a woman guest at the Quinta dressed so casually in a wrap and wandering in the grounds so early.

Mindful of the toboggan run later, Diane put on a trouser suit in a shade of avocado green, a colour that suited her coppery hair. Dwight arrived on time in a big hired car and looked her over appraisingly.

'The weather has favoured us this morning,' he remarked cheerfully with a grin as he started the car. 'I don't see how it could have been any other with you looking like a million dollars.'

'You don't look too bad yourself,' Diane replied teasingly as she settled down into the roomy seat. His expensive summer weight suit in mistletoe gaberdine and his hand-made soft leather sandals were extremely smart.

Monte was about two thousand feet up and roughly half an hour's run in the car from Funchal. Diane found it delightful in a setting of pine and chestnut enriched by fresh scented breezes. Dwight parked the car and the fun began. The toboggan run over the cobbles had to be taken with a sense of adventure to be enjoyed. It proved rather hazardous and Diane spun round like a top on occasions during the descent, but she loved every moment of it.

Before going back to the car they had a coffee on the way at a small café, and then explored the Church of Our

Lady of Monte with its picturesque white towers looking enchanting against the plane trees. Dwight suggested lunch at the charming village of Santana and they took once more to the road.

The way ahead curved steeply and they were soon among wild rugged country of mountain gorges and high spiky crags. On closer acquaintance, Diane saw that the mountains had been hewn out in terraces to bear crops. There were flowers everywhere and lots of camellias heavy with scarlet blossom. Half way to Santana Dwight stopped the car for them to walk a short way to stand on the famous Balcão, a natural plateau of rock perched balcony-wise two thousand feet above a great ravine. One had to have a head for heights to enjoy it.

Diane was enchanted with Santana and loved the quaint thatched-roofed houses looking like something out of a Hans Andersen story. The thatch continued right down to the ground serving as an added protection against the fierce winter gales from the Atlantic that swept the island. High hedges of hydrangeas served the same purpose, hugging gardens overflowing picturesquely with beans, peas, peaches, plums, apples, pumpkins, maize and camellias.

The inn where they stopped for lunch was white and weatherbeaten. One entered by a courtyard containing a massive magnolia tree. Inside the dining room they sat at a table decorated with flowers and beautifully clean. The meal was excellent and from where Diane sat there was the sound of a babbling stream.

'Like another world, isn't it?' she remarked dreamily across the table at her companion. They were lingering over their excellent coffee. 'I can imagine it was something like dropping off a roundabout to you after the busy lift in the States?'

Dwight sat back contentedly in his chair and lighted a cigar. 'In a way. I never guessed it would turn out to be so lucky for me.'

Diane surveyed him levelly over the top of her coffee. 'Lucky? How come?'

'Meeting you, of course. You've proved to be the tonic I needed.'

Diane smiled. 'You mean after losing the yacht race. Will your father mind?'

'Who told you about my father?'

'The Duque. He said your father and his mother are great friends.'

Dwight agreed, and gazed thoughtfully at the glowing end of his cigar.

'What did he say about me?' he queried slowly.

'Nothing.' Diane's eyes began to twinkle. 'Come to think of it, he did warn me to take care when I told him you were taking me out.'

'Did he now?' he drawled. 'I wonder why.'

Diane shrugged. 'He'd been warning me about staying too long in the sun.'

He narrowed his eyes through the cigar smoke at the smart little triangle of scarf knotted at the back of her head. 'Pity to cover that copper nob of yours. Did he say when his sister is due back?'

'Soon, I believe.'

'Doesn't it strike you as odd that she wasn't here to welcome you when you arrived? After all, you came at her invitation.'

'Not really. You see, the invitation was given months before I decided to accept it. I came on the spur of the moment and Maria had made other plans.'

'Which she could have cancelled. It was a special occasion, meeting you after all these years of corresponding.'

Diane wanted to agree with him. It would have been nice to confide in him about the Duque's attitude to her visit, but her word had been given to say nothing to anyone. Diane was not a person to go back on her word, so she just smiled and said lightly, 'The important thing is that Maria invited me.'

'I agree,' he said. 'What do you think of the Duque's girl-friend, Bella Vangroot? I'd say she had her eye on the main chance there.' He chuckled 'I wish you could have seen the contrast your copper nob made against her black one. Mind you, while I'm all in favour of the peaches and cream complexion, her magnolia one was quite something against those black eyes.'

Diane said carefully, 'The Duque is distantly related to her. Tell me about the yacht race. Was it very gruelling?'

He smiled at the swift change of conversation but let it pass. 'Not really. Dad was going to take part, but a touch of arthritis stopped him from doing so. He reckoned it was politic to stay away from the damp atmosphere of the sea until he was better.'

Diane nodded. 'He was wise, although he'll probably say you lost the race because he wasn't there.'

Dwight laughed. 'You would like him. He's a good sort, even if he is always telling me that I'm lazy and will never amount to anything.'

His expression softened as he went on to tell her amusing little anecdotes about his old man and Diane could see that they were very close. She could also see that Dwight junior was the kind of person who never allowed anything to disturb him very much. It did not take much imagination to see that he would eventually be ruled by the woman he married. However, one could be wrong. One thing was certain, Diane liked men to be a little more determined, like—the Duque. His lazy exterior masked an iron will. Now why should she think of the Duque? Surely it was time to do that when she met him again. Strangely enough, she found herself looking forward to it.

It was after eleven when Dwight delivered her at the Quinta de Valmardi after finishing off the day by dining with his host and hostess at the Villa Rosa, about twenty minutes' drive away. She was tired and even a little light-headed, which she put down to the surfeit of fresh air in a high altitude. Ten minutes later she was in bed and fast asleep. She awoke around midnight with severe pains in her stomach. Her forehead was clammy and damp, yet her whole body felt on fire.

She lay bearing the violent spasms of pain racking her body until she was bathed in sweat and almost delirious. It would not be fair to ring for Sofia, who would by this time be fast asleep, but she had to do something to stop the pain. Her one thought was to seek relief from a hot drink in the kitchen. The floor seemed hinged as she left her bed and struggled into her wrap, then stumbled across the floor to the door.

There wasn't a sound when she switched on the corridor wall lights, and gripped the balustrade on her way downstairs. The stairs seemed to go on and on, but at last her foot touched the hall floor. It was then that a sudden spasm of pain tore right through her. Sweat oozed out of her as she grabbed the carved post at the foot of the balustrade in an effort to stop herself from fainting. With her arms around it and her hot forehead pressed against the cool wood she felt her strength going, and gradually she found herself sinking down, down to the floor.

She was vaguely aware of firm footsteps followed by a muttered exclamation. Then she was being swept up into strong arms and borne away as on a blessed soft cloud before oblivion claimed her.

Diane opened her eyes through mists of pain to find herself lying in her bed. Turning her head, she saw the long brown hand and tapering fingers resting on the arm of a chair near her. The arm was perfectly still, as was the tall figure sitting there. Oh dear, she thought. It would be the Duque!

'How are you feeling?' His deep voice roused her into lifting her eyes to his face. The bedside light was on, throwing the clear cut lines into shadow so that his expression was unreadable. Then his cool hand was on her forehead and Diane closed her eyes again from his intent look.

'I—I don't know,' she confessed, holding herself tense in readiness for the next spasm of pain.

'I do,' he answered. 'You are feeling like death. Is that not so?'

She nodded and swallowed, not daring to move, as he went on.

'You have what we call Madeira fever. Many visitors succumb to this and spend an unpleasant day or so until they recover. It is something to do with the sun, a surfeit of fruit, wine and rich food to which the stomach is not accustomed. I am now going to give you a dose of a very unpleasant mixture which will work miracles in getting you well again.' His arm was sliding under her as he spoke and lifting her up to a sitting position. Then he was turning round to pick something up from the bedside table. 'Open your mouth and let it go down quickly. You will hardly know that you have taken it.'

It was a dark disgusting mixture, but Diane swallowed it gallantly. He held her up for a few moments to allow her to swallow it properly, then gently he laid her down again.

'Your first meeting with a brew called Fernet Branca,' he said as she quelled a shudder. 'You have been very brave.'

Then he rose slowly to his feet. He said quietly, 'Sofia will be with you during the night. Tomorrow, if you are no better, I will summon the doctor.' He laid the back of a cool hand on her hot forehead. 'Fortunately these attacks are of short duration. A day of complete rest will do much for your recovery.'

But Diane was past hearing him. The horrible mixture he had poured down her throat was beginning to explode inside her, filling her mouth with fumes, and she wanted to die. During the night she had to leave her bed many times to go to the bathroom, helped by a sympathetic Sofia. It was not much after dawn when she fell into a sleep of utter exhaustion.

It was midday when she awoke feeling exhausted, feverish and very weak. Sofia sponged her down, and changed the bed linen, then put her into fresh, clean pyjamas.

'The Senhor Duque has been in several times to see you and the doctor has also been,' Sofia said as she gathered the soiled linen together to be laundered. 'You would like a little soup?'

Diane quelled a shudder at the mention of food. 'No, thanks. A drink is all I want. What did the doctor say?'

Sofia shrugged. 'You are improving. He agreed with the Senhor Duque that you have Madeira fever. Now I will fetch you some coffee.'

The coffee was laced with brandy—on the orders of the Duque, Sofia said. Diane drank it thirstily and felt the friendly warmth seeping through her. Five minutes later she was asleep again. It was evening when she awoke and the curtains had been drawn together. The bedside lamp was on and she was aware of someone in the room.

'You feel a little better? How are the pains? Gone, I trust?'

Alonso was bending over her with concern and she looked up at him dazedly.

'The pains have gone, at least for the time being,' she admitted on a pale smile. 'I'm awfully sorry to cause all this trouble.'

He clicked his fingers disdainfully in the air. 'No apology is needed. It is just one of those things. Unfortunately that potent brew I gave you was necessary to rid your system of the upset. Terrible, was it not?' He gave a half smile. 'Nevertheless it did the trick. The good doctor left some sleeping pills which I decided were unnecessary since you seemed to have slept without them. You appear to have a healthy constitution despite your frail appearance.'

'I've never been ill in my life,' she said, 'apart from an attack of measles when I was at school. Poor Sofia, I'm afraid I kept her up for most of last night.'

'Sofia went to bed shortly after you went off to sleep this morning. And now I want you to take a little nourishment to prevent that sinking feeling which so often cramps an empty stomach. You have eaten nothing since last night.'

Diane could not have cared less. A horrible numb feeling, a kind of respite between bouts of pain, had left her feeling suspended in an empty void. Even Alonso's magnetic presence for once failed to arouse her. It did occur to her, though, that he must have slipped into her room many times during the past twenty-four hours, and his suggestion about taking light nourishment was sensible. Minutes after he had left the room an elderly woman member of the staff came in with a steaming bowl of something like beef tea. Diane managed half of it and lay back against her pillows waiting for the inevitable pains. None came, and she drifted off to sleep.

She slept through the night and awoke to a beautiful day of brilliant sunshine. Sofia had not yet put in an appearance, and feeling much better, Diane decided to summon enough energy to take a shower and dress. It was surprising how weak she felt, but the operation was carried out successfully in between short rests on her bed while dressing. As she did so a glimpse or two in her dressing table mirror shook her considerably. Not only did she look washed out, her hair had lost its sheen, and she had not the energy nor the will to brush it back.

Sofia came rushing in when she was ready and dressed, full of apologies for oversleeping. She hoped the *senhorita* would forgive her, but she had called in during the night once or twice to find her sleeping. However, she was sure that the Senhor Duque would be displeased at her leaving her bed so soon.

'But I wanted to get up, Sofia,' Diane said firmly, feeling better every minute. 'I'd like some dry toast and some coffee, please, and I shall eat it sitting by my window looking at that gorgeous view.'

So Diane had her way and sat by the open window and enjoying the fresh sweet perfume of the flowers and the songs of the birds. Thank goodness the pains in her stomach had not returned, she thought with an inward shudder. They had been fairly volcanic. The fingers of dry toast took an age to swallow, but the coffee was delicious and she found herself gradually enjoying it.

Sofia was going out with the breakfast tray when the Duque walked in.

'And how are you this morning?'

Diane was hardly aware of the question, she was conscious only of Alonso towering above her. He wore a white

56

silk shirt with a tan silk scarf tucked elegantly into the neck opening and immaculate beige slacks belted through loops around his waist. But his elegant appearance did not detract from the element of almost pagan masculinity which he undoubtedly appeared to convey.

It was not only those black eyes looking down on her so critically; Diane felt definitely ten times weaker against his sparkling fitness, a fitness that was the result of long hours outdoors at his favourite pursuits, swimming, yachting, absorbing the sun and clean air, keeping moderation in all things. That deep penetrating gaze spoke of a man fully in command of his every action.

'I feel much better, Senhor Duque,' she said. 'Who could not, on such a beautiful morning? And do you know what?' Her eyes suddenly widened as though still unable to take in what she was going to tell him. Her laugh was a tinkle of pure delight and a gleam came momentarily into his eyes. 'I thought the camellia tree had changed colour. But it hasn't. It's turned a bright yellow because it's full of canaries. I never heard such singing.'

'They probably came to sing because they are pleased to see you up again. We take such things for granted. However, that does not mean that we do not appreciate them. Sofia tells me that you have managed a little breakfast. That is very sensible. There will be light refreshment for you at intervals now to build up your strength again!' He paused thoughtfully, then went on, 'It will be a nice change for you to sit on the terrace until lunch time, if you feel up to it. I will have one of the loungers brought from the swimming pool to ensure that you will be comfortable.'

Diane grew a little agitated at the thought that he might be thinking of keeping her company.

'Please don't bother,' she hastened to say. 'I'm perfectly happy here in my room, thanks all the same.'

His eyes narrowed down at her pale face. 'Come now, I am sure you will enjoy it. It will not be any—er—bother.'

Diane loved his slight hesitation over the unfamiliar word and his sudden smile melted her bones. What was the

57

matter with her? Could an attack of Madeira fever make one weak in the head because she was beginning to find the arrogant Alonso quite lovable?

She looked helplessly at the back of his wide shoulders as he addressed one of the gardeners from the open window down below.

'Tomás,' he was saying, 'a lounger from the swimming pool to put on the terrace. *Depressoa, se faz favor!*' He was smiling when he turned round. 'Take my arm. You will feel weak for a while. The fresh air from a sheltered corner of the terrace will revive your flagging spirits. After lunch will be time enough for you to return to your room.'

He took her hand as she stood up and tucked it into the crook of his arm. None of this could, she felt, be real. There was a dreamlike quality about it. The hot colour rushed to her cheeks and she covered her confusion as best she might. However, a quick look at his proud arrogant profile told her that any emotion was all on her side. Until now they had remained almost strangers, exchanging the kind of remarks that politeness demanded. As far as the Duque de Valmardi was concerned. Diane McNair was a pen-friend of his sister, and a rather unwelcome one at that. But to Diane it was not like that at all—not now. Alonso was growing to be more important to her. There was a reason for her reactions to his presence. It was obvious that she ought not to stay on any longer at the Quinta because it could mean danger, yet how could she leave without causing embarrassment? She ought to have left when he first made his opinion of her clear. However, it was too late for that. Whatever kind of departure she decided upon now would, at the least, appear clumsy and rude. No, whatever the outcome of her visit she was committed to it.

After all, she thought reasonably, I am Maria's friend and and I owe it to her to wait until she arrives. Besides, they had a little sorting out to do over the matter of Alonso and his reactions to her photograph. Maria had obviously made up the story. But why? It was something she had to find out. At least she knew that Alonso's powerful attraction was something to fear and to steer clear of. The worst of it was that she did not want to do either. But there was no choice.

She decided a dip in the swimming pool would do her no harm. She found her swimming things and swam gently. Her thoughts still disturbed her and pulling herself up out of the water, she sat for a while on the side of the pool, taking off her bathing cap and raking her hand through the flattened copper hair. The silence beneath a shimmering blue sky broken only by the song of birds was almost profound, so much so that the sound of a car arriving at the Quinta, followed by voices, came very clearly to her ears. Bella Vangroot was not one of them and there were more than two voices. Rising hurriedly to her feet, Diane was about to sprint along the side of the pool to where her wrap had been discarded when a small group of people came around the wall of poinsetta and bougainvillaea.

Diane stood poised for flight and stared nonplussed to see Alonso with a man and two women coming towards the pool. Suddenly the dark young woman of the group ran forward eagerly.

'Diane!' she cried. ' I knew you would be lovely because your letters were. How wonderful to see you at last. Please forgive me for not being here, but I . . .' She paused breathlessly, then rushed on, 'What does it matter? What does anything matter now that you are here!'

Diane, waiting with amusement and affection for the girl to stop talking, knew that this lovely creature could only be Maria, Alonso's sister, who, for all her reserved upbringing, was as excited as a child. The lovely dark eyes set in an oval face of pure magnolia smoothness were dancing with delight.

They clasped hands and Diane leaned forward to kiss the smooth perfumed cheek. 'It's lovely to see you too, Maria. But I must put on my wrap—if you will excuse me while I fetch it,' she said warmly.

Before she could do so, however, someone spoke at her elbow.

'Welcome to the Quinta de Valmardi, Diane, although my greeting is a little belated. I'm Maria's mother. I trust Alonso has been looking after you during our absence.'

The twinkling brown eyes of the older woman were looking with approval at Diane's slender shapely figure in the blue swimsuit before travelling up to the disordered copper-coloured hair rioting in glorious confusion around her flushed face.

'The Duque has been wonderfully kind,' she said, aware of that tall figure now somewhere in the vicinity. 'I must apologise for you finding me like this. If you will excuse me I'll fetch my wrap.'

The next moment the wrap was placed on her shoulders from behind and held there by firm hands. Blindly Diane thrust her arms into the sleeves and hurriedly fumbled for the cord to tie around her waist. The quick glance upwards at Alonso's dark face was brief.

'Thank you,' she said.

He gave a polite inclination of the head and said smoothly, 'May I present Maria, my sister, my mother and Senhor Felipe Moltardo. Felipe is an old friend of the family.'

Felipe! To Diane the name rang a bell. Felipe? Of course, the man Alonso wanted Maria to marry. She was aware of all things at once—Alonso's mocking smile, the two lovely women whom she was sure to adore and the dishy young man smiling at her so appraisingly with warm blue eyes in a strong-boned good-looking face.

He held out a strong hand and clasped hers warmly. 'I've been looking forward to meeting you, Miss McNair,' he said in English. 'Maria has told me so much about you. My mother was English, so we have a little in common.'

They all strolled back to the Quinta, where Diane excused herself to go to her room and change.

'Miss McNair!'

Diane was pulled up short at the foot of the staircase to find Alonso at her elbow. The others had presumably gone into the *sala* to take refreshment after their journey and they were quite alone in the hall.

'Your bathing cap,' he said, handing it to her.

For a moment Diane felt herself held by that intent dark gaze. The air seemed charged with electricity as she took the cap, but the next second it changed. He was unsmiling and she borrowed some of his coolness.

'Thanks,' she said briefly, and turned away.

He put a hand on her arm. 'Now that Maria is home I think it is time for you and me to dispense with formality. From now on the Senhor Duque will be Alonso. I may call you Diane?'

His smile was a polite one suitable for the query and Diane froze. If he had been a little more friendly her answer would have come spontaneously. As it was, he was letting her know it was something he was forced to accept, like her presence at the Quinta.

She turned round slowly to face him. 'I see what you mean,' she answered in a cold little voice. 'It would seem odd, wouldn't it, for you and me to continue being so formal. But at least it would be honest, knowing how you feel about me and my presence here. Call me whatever you wish. I'm sure you always do what you want.'

She went quickly up the stairs. How dared he tell her what to call him? His name would stick in her throat in any case because there would be nothing of friendship in it. She would not put it past him to tell his girl-friend to use christian names when next meeting Miss McNair. That would be too funny. Bella treating her like a friend with a honeyed voice and small daggers in her dark eyes. Diane chided herself in minding so much what Alonso and his girl-friend did. Now Maria was back there would be ample opportunity to avoid them except at meal times, and then there would be other people present.

She was trembling as she reached her room. Her throat was dry and her eyes were pricked by tears. To think that she had arrived on the island with the idea that Alonso was in love with her photograph! Her hands clenched as she walked across her room to gaze out unseeingly through the open window. Why was she so angry with Alonso? Was it because of his complete detachment—the cold way that he disapproved of her. Of Maria she could not think beyond the sudden shock of discovering how she had deceived her. Even then at the time it had not seemed important, and there had to be a reason why Maria had done what she had. No, it was Alonso she blamed, and her whole being urged her to go home and set about planning her future.

When the thought of how nice Maria and her mother had been came to her she thrust it away and covered her face with her hands despairingly. It was the thought of Alonso which dominated her—his strength, his consideration, his concern when she was ill and, above all, his tenderness. Oh yes, he could be tender and loving too. But he had no illusions about herself. Then she must have no illusions about him. She knew what his power over her senses could still be, and she had to fight it for all she was worth until her visit came to an end.

CHAPTER FOUR

DIANE had discarded her swimsuit, spent a few minutes under the shower to wash the pool water from her skin, towelled herself dry, and was standing in bra and panties when a knock came on her door and Maria entered. She paused in the doorway to watch Diane put on a wrap, then came forward eagerly into the room to sit down on a damask-covered chair.

'I really cannot believe that you are here!' she exclaimed, then, bending forward conspiratorially, her eyes dark with mischief, she said, 'Well, what do you think of Alonso? Do you think you can take him from that odious Bella?'

Diane leaned back against the dressing table, feeling in need of support. She had been thinking of a way to approach Maria on the subject of her brother, and here she was coming right to the point in such a disarming way that it was difficult to be angry with her as she had every right to be.

'Ah yes,' she replied, eyeing the lovely face sternly. 'I really ought to be very angry with you for making up that ridiculous story about your brother falling in love with my photograph. It isn't true, is it?'

Maria looked sheepish and spread her small hands palms upwards in a gesture of guilty resignation. Somewhat reluctantly, she said, 'Not exactly. I had to do something to persuade you to come. You have always refused my invitations, so I thought you would be intrigued enough to come and see the charming young man who had fallen in love with your photograph.'

Diane stared at her aghast. Maria was not the slightest bit put out by her deception.

'But don't you see,' she argued, 'how embarrassing it would have been for your brother if he knew, and embarrassing for me too. I could easily have let it slip when he met me what I believed to be true.'

Maria looked resentful. 'You put it so crudely, Diane, as though I had told a deliberate lie. And it was not so. I am sure that Alonso liked your photograph.'

'Did he say so?'

'No,' Maria admitted reluctantly. 'But when I showed him your photograph in order that he might recognise you when he went to meet you a funny thing happened. He was silent.'

Diane said dryly, 'And I suppose he communicated his thoughts to you by telepathy?'

Maria shook her head. 'Usually when Alonso sees a photograph he passes some remark, possibly a dry one, but a remark Your photograph must have made him speechless, because he did not say a word.'

Diane thrust her arms mandarin-fashion into the wide sleeves of her wrap Her tones were heavy with sarcasm. 'You mean my beauty took away his power of speech?' she said scornfully.

'Yes, that was it,' Maria cried triumphantly. 'Otherwise he would have said something.'

Diane had to laugh, it was so ridiculous. 'My dear Maria,' she said soberly, 'I'm a very ordinary young woman and I'm certainly not a Helen of Troy. Your brother is a man of the world who has seen many beautiful women. As I certainly don't class myself as one of them don't you think you could be indulging in a light fantasy where your brother and I are concerned? And what's all this nonsense about you refusing to marry Felipe because you're under the impression that you're being forced into it?'

'But I am,' Maria protested indignantly.

'You mean your family want you to marry him?'

She nodded. 'Alonso wants to see me married before he gets married himself.'

Diane digested this and wished she did not find it so unpalatable.

'You're forgetting the most important thing, Maria. Does

Felipe want to marry you because he loves you?' she asked wistfully.

'Felipe loves me. He is crazy about me.' Maria sighed. 'I used to be very jealous of my sister Francine because I thought she was in love with Felipe. They are the same age, twenty-eight. But Francine married a fellow student of Alonso's and they lived in Portugal. Her husband is now a *conde*.'

Diane spoke as if being reasonable against her will. 'Why didn't you tell me your brother is a *duque*?'

Maria stared at her with wide-eyed innocence. 'I suppose I never really thought about it. Does it matter? Anyway, he only became a *duque* because a distant cousin died without an heir and Alonso was the next in line. Our father did not bear the title.'

Diane smiled. 'Not really. What does matter is you refusing to marry the man that you love just to spite your brother.'

Maria lifted her chin militantly. 'I am going to teach my brother that he cannot order me around and have things all his own way. If I have to be married first then he can wait to get married. Besides . . .' she broke off as though she had said too much.

'Go on,' said Diane. 'I'm your friend.'

'I was going to say why should I marry Felipe and let Alonso marry Bella? I hate her. She has always had her eyes on Alonso, and has always played up to him. I know that several men have made her offers of marriage, but she refused them.'

'What if she's genuinely in love with your brother? It's quite possible. And if your brother is in love with her there's nothing that you can do about it.'

Maria looked at her hopefully. 'But you can. You are so lovely and she is so hard and calculating. Alonso is no fool. You could do it, I know you could. Bella has her eye on bigger fish. Her other suitors were not wealthy and they had no title. Don't you see?'

If Diane did she was determined not to say. The worst

thing that could happen was for her to be drawn into family troubles. Neither had she any intention of telling Maria her brother's feelings towards herself. Maria would not be within confessing to him her perfidy and this would make it impossible for Diane to stay at the Quinta. Not that she intended to stay long. Better to say nothing and cut her visit short now that she knew everything.

Gently she said, 'This is a special day for us, Maria. We've met for the first time after writing to each other all those years. I don't know about you, but I feel I've known you all my life. Don't let anything spoil it.'

Maria was visibly moved. 'You are right. We will not spoil it, this very special day. But tell me, Diane, would you marry Alonso if he asked you? Just think, you would be my beloved sister for always.'

Diane laughed helplessly. 'Oh, Maria, what am I to do with you? Do you never give up? Darling, I met your brother for the first time only a matter of days ago. One doesn't fall in love at the first polite greeting, not even an English girl. It takes time.'

But did it? Diane was asking herself the question with inward tremors. She did love Alonso, loved him deeply. She had fallen in love with the beauty of the island, the flowers, the trees, the picturesque cultured mountains, and then gradually with Alonso. It had happened on the day that he had suggested her sitting on the terrace after her illness. He had hesitated boyishly over the word 'bother' with an endearing smile. The small gesture had winged its way to her heart and she had wanted to hug him. It was the reason why the thought of him marrying Bella was so unbearable.

Maria was saying rather petulantly, 'You sound so practical, as though your head ruled your heart, and I know this is not so. I . . .'

She broke off at a tap on the door. 'Time to dress for dinner, girls.'

At the sound of her mother's voice, Maria rose reluctantly to her feet. Her dark eyes entreated. 'We will talk again soon,' she said, and left the room.

They met in the corridor on their way downstairs. Maria was dressed in cream lace with picot-edged square neck and bell sleeve cuffs. A cream lace bow was pinned at the back of her chignon of black hair and a jewelled necklace around her slim throat matched the drop ear-rings.

She looked petite, chic and delightful, thought Diane, with her dainty hands and feet and her erect graceful carriage. But if she was admiring her friend, Maria was admiring her too.

'You look young, fresh and sweet, and I love your dress,' she exclaimed, looking with admiration at the gossamer-fine cream jersey dress with its enchanting design of blue, coral and green in fondant colours. 'And your pretty coral necklace and ear-studs are a perfect match. You are going to turn many male heads.'

Diane laughed. 'Thanks,' she replied. 'If I do they'll only be staring curiously at a stranger in their midst. I've never had men swooning at my feet. What about you? I'm sure you have.'

Maria said primly, 'It is not becoming to talk about male admirers. We are taught to behave with a certain amount of decorum.'

'Yet you expect me to be different in the way of attracting the opposite sex. Why?'

'Because you are English and free to do as you please, even to choosing a husband for yourself.'

'But we don't actually choose our own husbands. In fact they choose us. They do the proposing, Maria. We only decide whether to accept or not.'

'And that is what I want, to be free to accept or not. Do you not see? I want to be like you.'

So it was out. Maria had been influenced by her letters. Alonso had been right. A swift glance at her friend's set little profile confirmed that she meant what she said. Something other than English influence was called for.

Carefully Diane said, 'I don't know why you should want to be like me when you have a perfectly dishy man at your feet. Yes, I mean Felipe.' She smiled as Maria looked at her curiously. 'Let him loose in London and he would soon be breaking hearts wherever he went.'

Maria pouted. 'I refuse to be pushed into marriage. I can see that my brother has you on his side.'

'Don't be absurd, Maria. Just because I admire Felipe it doesn't mean that I'm pushing him on to you. In any case, I'm glad you're free at the moment so that we can spend a lovely time together. There is one thing, though, that I feel I must say before we close the matter of Felipe once and for all. Don't keep him dangling too long, because someone else might come along and snap him up.'

Conversation ended as they reached the *sala*. Alonso was there, immaculate in evening dress, pouring out drinks while he talked to Felipe who was accepting one. Looking at the black hair trimmed neatly against the deep tan of his face Diane was still uncertain of herself, a contradiction against and for this man who held her heart in those long tapering hands. His smile was her undoing. It lifted her heart. It was challenging and magnetic as he saw them enter, yet strangely remote as those dark eyes rested momentarily on her face.

'Ah, you could not have timed it better,' he said in his deep pleasant voice in English. 'This is a special occasion, so we must all drink to it, this meeting of two kindred souls for the first time.' And to Felipe, who stood quietly by, 'And so alike in build that they might be sisters. Would you agree, Felipe?'

Felipe gave a dazzling smile, put down his glass on the mantelpiece and came forward to seat the two girls in comfortable velvet-covered chairs.

'I certainly would. Both so lovely, one with hair as black as night, the other whose tresses rival a Madeira sunset,' he said with a grin.

Diane, looking at his appraising smile, felt it would be easy to like him. He had a boyish appeal in marked contrast to the more arrogant Alonso who was bending over her with a glass of champagne. The charm was visible in his smile, so was the ruthlessness noticeable at close quarters in the

68

mobile mouth and firm determined jaw.

The dark gaze was baffling as he said dryly, 'We will all drink a toast to your visit to the Quinta.'

When the glass changed hands, his fingers touched her own, and Diane found the contact with their firmness oddly disturbing. Her hand trembled a little and in the next second his mother entered the room. She looked much younger than her age in a blue dress which did much for her fair hair.

Alonso was now pouring out more champagne. 'We are about to propose a toast, Mother, to Miss McNair's visit,' he told her smoothly.

She came gracefully across the room to pause beside the two girls before going to sit on the chaise-longue at the other side of the fireplace. She really was very attractive, Diane thought. The contrast of dark brown eyes set in a fair skin and golden hair with a fine sprinkling of grey gave her an undimmed beauty which some women carry untouched through the years.

'We must give a party very soon, Alonso. Many of our friends will be thrilled to meet Maria's friend.' She smiled down warmly at the two young faces and addressed Diane. 'They're most interested and intrigued by your friendship with my daughter. Francine, my elder daughter, particularly wanted to see you, but she had to return home a few weeks ago after a visit to the Quinta.'

Making her way to the chaise-longue, she accepted a glass of champagne from her son. The toast was drunk with Alonso proposing it, and Diane avoiding his slightly sardonic smile. She could not remember anyone disliking nor disapproving anything about her before, and to find it in a practical stranger like Alonso was disconcerting to say the least. But then his mother with her gracious welcome and Maria more than made up for the son of the house and his antagonism. Thank goodness Felipe was inclined to be friendly, and he was so obviously in love with Maria that his glances her way brought a lump to Diane's throat. A love like that belonged only to a chosen few. Maria did not

69

know how lucky she was, and her brother by the very force of his personality was probably going to be the one who would be responsible for them not coming together.

Contrary to her expectations the meal went smoothly. Coffee and liqueurs were served on the terrace for the three women while the two men enjoyed their cheroots in the *sala*. Felipe, however, did not stay long. He appeared both anxious and reluctant to be off. Poor boy, Diane thought. Maria did not look his way even when he was taking his leave, but she made no demur when her mother suggested they go to see Felipe to his car.

His smile at Diane as he bade her farewell was friendly and warm.

'I would deem it an honour,' he said politely, 'if you would come to my home and meet my family. Had you arrived earlier you could have accompanied Maria—but no matter. We will look upon it as a pleasure to look forward to.'

'You have made a conquest with Felipe,' Alonso said softly above her ear. 'What did you think of him?'

Diane had been left to herself on the terrace while Felipe said his goodbyes to Maria and her mother outside in the warm night, and she had gone to stand by the balustrade to look out on the view of twinkling lights over the bay. Alonso's voice had taken her unawares and she turned to find herself facing him. Against her will she noticed how well cut his mouth was, how firm although slightly cynical at the moment. She looked steadily at him, then turned towards the balustrade of the terrace before answering. Her pulses were hammering and her breathing was constricted by his nearness.

'I thought him perfectly charming,' she answered as steadily as she could.

'A suitable match for Maria?' he mocked.

'That is for Maria to decide,' she answered coldly.

'Is it, Diane? You could help her to decide.'

He had moved beside her. She saw his lean brown hand on the rail not far from her clenched white one. It looked strong and ruthless.

'Maria could decide herself if you left her alone,' she said coolly. His use of her name had shaken her and she decided to ignore it.

'You mean wait for the knight on the white charger to come and rescue her from her big bad brother?' he scoffed.

Diane's fingers tightened on the balustrade, aching to slap his dark mocking face. She did not answer.

'You are as naïve as she is if you believe that,' he jeered.

'Then I can't do her much harm if I'm naïve, can I?'

She lifted her chin and her eyes blazed at him as she turned round. He was unperturbed. His voice was maddeningly casual.

'On the contrary, you have influenced Maria a great deal and you can now influence her from indulging in her dreams. If you wish to.'

Diane bit on her lip. He was baiting her and she knew it. Anger steadied her limbs and her voice.

Quietly, she said, 'Neither you nor I can keep Maria from her dreams. In any case, despite your cynicism regarding romance your own ancestors obviously believed in it. The fact that one of them rode away with the maiden of his choice seems to have escaped your memory. You told me yourself that not only did he carry her off but he kept her a prisoner in the lodge in these very grounds.'

A few moments passed and he answered with cool amusement, 'Do you think it would help if I suggested to Felipe that he ride away with Maria? It is a point worth considering.'

He had not answered her question but had avoided it adroitly. It was something she expected of him, this command of every situation that might arise. A swift glance in his direction revealed the fact that he was staring across the gardens at the bay. His profile was clear cut against the gloom and he was smiling. Diane sizzled with anger, wishing she could pay him back with the same cutting sarcasm.

'I'm sure you would even do that if you thought that it would bring results,' she retorted. 'I . . .'

Whatever else was in her mind to say was never said, for Maria and her mother appeared on the terrace as the sound of Felipe's car roared away in the distance. The Senhora's smile was sweet.

'What a lovely night,' she remarked. 'Far too lovely to go to bed, yet I am all for it. Travel tires one.'

'I will come with you,' Diane said swiftly. It was imperative for her to get away from Alonso just then and she was in no mood to have any further discussion with Maria that night. To her relief both women accompanied her to go to their rooms.

Diane stood at her window for a long time. Nothing had been as she had expected it—except Maria, of course. Her letters had revealed the kind of person she was, sweet and kind and very much like herself in some ways. Her mother had been a lovely surprise. There was no doubt in her mind that she was going to like her. But Alonso was a different kettle of fish. But this was Madeira, an island thirty-eight miles long and fifteen miles wide with a craggy backbone of mountains running from east to west. From these, glens cleaved their way down to the shores. A rugged country sufficient unto itself, like Alonso, and just as difficult to know.

She thought of the brown, sinewy men carrying heavy loads on shoulders that hardly stooped to bear them, the women daintily carrying baskets of flowers on their heads and the laughing children hiding behind their skirts and peeping at strangers as they passed. There was a dignity about them, not a disdainful dignity but one born of contentment and happiness in the hard work that was so essential to their livelihood and wellbeing. They were not only industrious, their lives were filled with purpose based on echoes of the past which still lived in the mountains, valleys, small fishing villages and bustling towns. And everywhere there was beauty, the beauty of contentment on the brown faces, the beauty of green strips of land, the beauty of lush vegetation, the beauty of mountains emerging from scarves of mist in breathtaking colours, and the beauty of small villages which still retained the feudal air of the Quinta de Valmardi.

Diane felt the warmth of it all not only in the sun but in the warm smiles and greetings of the people, and she was beginning to love it. If only she had not fallen in love with Alonso! Pain, shattering and intolerable, rose from her heart. When she left the island it would mean severing the relationship with Maria, for it would be intolerable to hear from her all the details of his eventual marriage to Bella. It was inconceivable that she should come all this way to lose her heart to a man who had no use for it, heartbreaking also that it meant the loss of her friend.

Suddenly a red glow beneath her window caught her attention. Alonso was standing looking out over the bay, taking the cheroot from his mouth now and again to gaze at the tip as though deep in thought. With a lurch of her heart, Diane wondered what he was thinking, or better still, cooking up in that handsome head of his. With a wry smile she wished that the man he wanted Maria to marry was old and senile, then it would have given her immense satisfaction in disliking, even hating him. As it was, the fact that Felipe was young, good-looking and charming suggested a different person, a more human, sincere one who had the welfare of his sister at heart. He was, she decided, the most maddening man she had ever met.

The next few days proved to be utter bliss for Diane, from the first leisurely moment of wakening to the gradual drifting to bed at the end of a long full day of pleasure. It seemed to her that each pleasure was drained to the dregs before drifting on to the next.

The day began with breakfast on the terrace for the two girls, since Maria's mother preferred to breakfast in her room. They ate their fill of crisp warm rolls spread with farm butter and honey, and teetered between eggs and a large dish of fresh fruit while indulging in cups of delicious creamy coffee. Then they would flick through the magazines and daily papers, at least Diane did, while Maria read her mail.

Mindful of what Alonso had said about the power of the sun, Diane became acquainted with it gradually. She had

73

discovered that the best way to do so was sunbathing on the side of the pool in between dips in the water. The essential thing to remember was never to fall asleep when sunbathing. In the presence of Maria this was impossible, for she chatted on and on. Diane listened with amusement, allowing for the fact that when her sister Francine married, Maria must have missed her company very much

So, eyes closed, stretched out on her stomach with her face resting on her folded arms, Diane carried on a conversation with a similarly recumbent Maria. It was amazing how well they got on together, massaging each other with suntan lotion, giggling a lot and generally letting their hair down.

There were times, especially when their laughter rang out across the swimming pool, that Diane knew Alonso would not approve. But he was not at the Quinta. He had left on the day following Maria's arrival, and since he had gone the Quinta had not been the same. To Diane it had assumed a listening quality, a breathless waiting for his reappearance. She hungered for the sight of his lean, nonchalant figure, the mocking dark eyes and the scent of his cheroots which seemed to fill the whole Quinta with his presence.

Bella Vangroot had called at the Quinta one morning to pay her respects to the returning family. It was midmorning and she was entertained on the terrace by Maria's mother, who had been going through her morning mail. Before leaving she had come around the wall of plumbago in the garden to watch the two girls in the swimming pool. Maria had acknowledged her briefly with a cool, polite inclination of her head.

Bella's full lips had thinned and the dark eyes had cast a cursory glance at Diane's pretty figure in her swimsuit before taking her leave.

'I know why Bella has come,' Maria said crossly. They were back on their mattresses, stretched out to the sun. 'She knows Mother will be giving a party for you this weekend and she wants to be sure of being invited. Mother

74

does not like her much either, but all our relations and friends will be invited. Alonso returns home on Saturday, so Mother is arranging it for then.'

Diane said carefully, 'Will your Felipe be there?'

'He is not my Felipe. Really, Diane, you are as bad as Alonso! He continually refers to him as my Felipe.' Maria's voice had a distinct edge on it, but Diane only laughed.

The thought of Alonso returning at the weekend filled her with a tingling sense of happiness. On Friday morning Maria paid a visit to the dentist in Funchal. Diane went with her and strolled through the town while waiting for her. Happily she meandered through the market, hurrying past the stalls of fish containing unrecognisable sinister creatures slit open and unwashed to disclose their red insides. The display of fruit and flowers was fabulous and she loved the quaint shops selling about everything one could wish for in essentials. There were cobblers, tinsmiths, joiners, wine stores, all small beehives of industry teeming with life and healthy vigour. The pale colour-washed houses with balconies massed with flowers drowsy in the heat gave her a warm feeling of being at home.

A strange sense of timelessness took complete hold of her with a power she felt was too strong to resist. At the moment it was sufficient to feel the sun warm upon her face and eyelids, even if there was an element of danger in it. Did not her continued presence on the island spell danger for herself and her own peace of mind? Nevertheless, she was not ready yet to return to London. A glance at her watch told her it was time to seek out Maria and, hastening her steps, she made for the dentist in the town.

She was walking past a wine shop when someone remarkably like Maria sitting inside with a young man pulled her up sharp. The couple were talking together earnestly. At once Diane entered the shop and in that moment Maria lifted her head and saw her.

'Diane!' she exclaimed through suddenly pale lips. 'We arranged to meet at the dentist's. Have you forgotten?'

Diane thought quickly, if ever I've seen a frightened girl

I'm looking at one right now. The knowledge that Maria was trembling strengthened her voice and manner.

'I would have said that you had forgotten, Maria, since we agreed to meet at twelve precisely. It's that now,' she said lightly.

She was aware of Maria's companion saying something in a swift undertone in Portuguese to her and making a gesture towards herself both arrogant and dismissive. His eyes, set close together, were as hard as flint as they raked Diane's face before returning to the nonplussed Maria. She rose hurriedly and motioned to him to accompany her. As all three strolled from the shop, she smiled at Diane.

'This is Pedro Banalda. He ... used to work on our estate. We ... we met unexpectedly and we have been talking about old times,' she said.

Her small face wore an expression of utter numbness, Diane thought, and if they had been discussing old times then they could not have been very happy ones. There was an atmosphere which felt volcanic, to say the least, especially as Pedro Banalda did not even acknowledge her presence. He merely turned to Maria, who was walking between them, and said something fierce in Portuguese. Maria's placating reply was sweet and low against this guttural voice. Then in the sunlit street someone approached and stopped in front of them. Diane looked up, startled. It was Alonso.

'My car awaits, *senhoritas*,' he said with a deadly calm. 'Shall we go?'

His manner seemed to suggest that this meeting had been prearranged, and under his steely-eyed regard Maria was fast recovering her composure. Not so Diane. That he was enraged there was no denying. His dark eyes burned into slits of rage and Diane, feeling the need of positive action, touched Maria's arm and they moved forward as he stood aside to let them.

'As for you, Banalda,' she heard him say, 'I shall thrash you within an inch of your life if you ever attempt to see my sister again.'

Maria did not speak. Her little face was set as they trod on the sunlit cobbles which struck hot to the feet through the soles of their sandals. But Diane felt borne along on wings. Alonso was back, and whatever scrape Maria had got into would soon be resolved by his timely arrival on the scene. It was inconceivable that Maria should have any liking for that awful young man. Granted, he was attractive in a Heathcliff kind of way, but it was in a nebulous form glossed over by the bloom of youth. When that faded there would be nothing left. Yet Maria did not appear to be relieved at her sudden release from his attentions, for she spoke no word to her brother when he joined them on the way to where their car was parked.

In the shade of palms Arnaldo, the chauffeur, leaned against the car which had brought them to Funchal and straightened smartly on seeing Alonso.

'Home at once, Arnaldo,' the Duque commanded in clipped tones, opening the door to the back seats for the two girls to slip inside.

He had not greeted Diane nor addressed her since his appearance, and if he had both shocked and hurt her by his sudden appearance and his manner, she was determined for it not to be transient. Before following Maria into the roomy interior, she took off her shady hat and shook out an escape for her soft curls. In outward appearance she was as cool and withdrawn as he was. He slid in beside Arnaldo and the car moved forward. Gradually the town slipped away and the car put on speed. Maria sat silent, pale and withdrawn as she stared through her window, leaving Diane free to look at the back of Alonso's well shaped head. It was impossible for her to know what was going on and, apart from the indignity of whispering to Maria, there was no way to find out. Poor Maria! She had evidently incurred her brother's wrath. Diane reached across the seat to clasp her friend's hand.

Marie's fingers curled around her warm ones, but her head was still turned towards the window. But by the time they had reached the Quinta de Valmardi, she had recovered enough to give Diane a warm smile. What her thoughts were Diane did not know, but her heart ached for her and the rather ruthless way her brother had intervened in a meeting which could not have been so important since it had taken place in daylight in a local wine shop. Come to think of it, Alonso had been very cool about it, although the man had been seething with indignation. But then he would never be at a loss in any situation.

At last the car was sliding to a halt outside the Quinta. Alonso extricated himself first and opened the car door for the two girls to get out.

Unsmiling, his dark eyes narrow and glittering, he addressed Maria.

'In the library, *por favor*, Maria,' he said peremptorily.

As Diane watched them walk together across the marble floor so cool and pleasant after the harsh hot cobbles of the town, she felt Alonso's anger as something tangible. It was a relief to go to her room and change for lunch.

In the library, Alonso indicated one of the deep velvet chairs for Maria to be seated and stood facing her with his back to the fireplace.

Looking very stern, he said coldly, 'I have never been so angry in my life. What were you thinking of to meet a man like Pedro Banalda, in a wine shop of all places, and alone? Where was your friend Diane?'

Maria sat with her hands folded in her lap and talked to them. 'Diane did not know anything about it. I had to go to the dentist for a check-up and I met Pedro accidentally.'

'You have met this man before without my knowledge?'

Maria gave a nervous little shrug. 'Several times, but never on my own account. He has always contrived a meeting.'

'And for what reason I can well arrive at. For money, was it not? How much have you given him, and when?' There was an uncomfortable silence and he repeated, 'How much did you give him? I can find out, but you must tell me yourself. Come on now, we have not all day to wait. Lunch will be ready soon.'

'Not much,' Maria admitted reluctantly. 'A few small cheques. You can check my bank book if you wish. I knew it was wrong, but I did feel a little bit guilty about his dismissal.'

'And why should you? The man had two months' salary in lieu of notice. He was the one to blame. He is years older than you are and while it was all innocent fun on your side, he had his eye on the main chance. I would not have employed him in the first place had you not insisted upon it. I also had a desire for you to study the man at close quarters and see for yourself what kind of a man he is. You know, of course, that he had already dishonoured one girl in the village. To think that a sister of mine should stoop to such a degrading level!'

'I am sorry, Alonso. But Pedro was such fun. He made me laugh—and do not forget he brought me home on that dreadful night of the storm. If he had not come across me when he did I might have perished.'

He gave a half smile and said sardonically, 'I doubt it. The most you would have suffered would have been a bad chill. In any case, Arnaldo had only run out of petrol and would not have been more than half an hour fetching more from the nearest garage. But no, you have to attempt to walk home.'

Maria wore a hurt expression. 'But, Alonso,' she pouted, 'I would have been back at the Quinta in less than that time taking that short cut in the hills had not the rain come.'

'Unfortunately Banalda came as well, sweeping you, a bedraggled maiden, up on his horse to bring you home. From then on you saw him as a laughing cavalier who had saved you from a fate worse than death instead of what he was, a lazy good-for-nothing skulking on his father's farm and pretending to work. It is time you stopped dreaming and faced up to realities. The man is no good—his own father admits it.'

Maria nodded. 'I know, but I thought if he had a chance to make good away from his family he would be a different man.'

Alonso's mouth thinned and he pushed his hands into his pockets with a gesture that indicated that the subject was becoming distasteful to him.

'The man has had endless chances. He lives for two things, gambling and women. This time I shall have him cleared off the island. Fortunately no harm has been done where you are concerned. You are lucky. I doubt if Felipe would have thought the same about you otherwise.'

Maria looked up at him in deep dismay. 'You mean you will tell him?' she said in a shocked whisper.

He gave a half smile. 'Do not look so shocked—nothing so terrible is going to happen.' He turned his wrist to consult his watch. 'Go along and change or you will be late for lunch.' His tones had softened, but he lifted an imperious hand. 'Before you go I want your promise that you will tell me immediately should Banalda attempt to contact you again.'

'I promise, Alonso, and I am sorry.' Maria went up on tiptoe to kiss his dark lean cheek, then turned slowly and left the room.

CHAPTER FIVE

THE party given for Diane at the Quinta was a glittering affair. The elaborately prepared table scintillated with silver, crystal glass and flower arrangements beneath ornate chandeliers no less brilliant than the gowns and jewels of the women present. The innumerable courses came and went, with Diane knowing that she could not eat the amount of food that seemed expected of her.

Alonso presided at the head of the table with his mother on one side and Maria on the other. He was drawing the guests into the charmed circle of his smile and wit. Diane, seated next to Maria, felt its power like a magnet. There was something about him that she could not resist, a kind of latent force reminiscent of the wild landscape of the island. It was there to stay, she knew. Nothing could undo it. Maria, bright and sparkling, chatted confidentially, going around the table and telling Diane who everyone was. She deliberately left out Bella, who was seated by her mother on the opposite side of the table. Like her brother, Maria had a ready wit and Diane was often convulsed at her gay repartee. She knew that this evening meant a great deal to both of them and that Maria was as happy as she was.

Felipe had not come as he was away on a visit to some relatives, but there were plenty of young men, some of them relatives of Maria, to dance with. Alonso had a warm, close, loving relationship with his mother. It showed in the attentive, amusing manner he undoubtedly used with her. During the meal Diane had set her mind and thoughts on Maria, but she receded perversely away. Alonso was the one who dominated her, and seemed more real.

Once when she had been laughing quietly at something Maria had said, his dark eyes had glanced her way. Her hair, curling softly away from her face, glowed beneath the lights which threw into relief the delicate bone structure, the broad forehead, widely-spaced dancing eyes and air of youthful exuberance. Diane hastily lowered her eyes. It had not been rudeness but a strange compelling unwillingness to lift the barrier which kept them as strangers. The same thing had happened again during the dancing.

Alonso had danced with his mother, Maria and Bella without approaching Diane until the evening was half way through. She had seen him coming to her, presumably for a dance, and she had more than half way met a young man with the same intention who had been much nearer. The impulsive action had not gone unnoticed by Alonso, and only an English girl would have dared to do such a thing to the Duque de Valmardi. His nostrils had thinned slightly and his face had set. So much for you, my girl, she had thought during the dance. He won't approach you again. A curious flatness fell on the evening as common sense told her this. It would have been better had she accepted and danced with him. There would have been an opportunity to see if the black magic of his nearness intensified. The mere thought of being in his arms made her tremble.

After the interval dancing had begun again and Diane was as usual surrounded by young men eager for her favours. Then somehow they divided into two camps and Alonso was in the centre. Without speaking he took her arm and led her among the dancers. Diane was just beginning to regain her breath to take in air normally when he guided her out of the room.

The whole incident had taken place so quickly that Diane was seated in the library before her senses were aware of what was happening.

'Since you appear to dislike the thought of dancing with me,' he was saying sardonically, 'we had better, as you say in England, sit this one out.' Dazedly Diane watched him pour out a glass of Madeira wine which he gave to her with the words. 'I want to talk to you.'

She did not want the wine, but it helped her to steady

her nerves as her hands cupped the base of the glass. It did not help to see him ledge himself against the edge of the heavily carved table confronting her. But it had to be said.

'I'm sorry,' she said quietly. 'I'm not going to excuse myself. I know you'll regard me as behaving very rudely, knowing that you were coming to request a dance. I didn't mean it to be. It—it just happened that way. You have only yourself to blame.'

'In what way?' he enquired coldly.

'Since you have made no secret of your dislike where I'm concerned you can hardly blame me. You were only going to ask me for a dance because it would be expected of you by your family.'

His voice was openly mocking. 'So you can read my thoughts?'

She shook her head. 'I don't think anyone can do that. You're much too enigmatic.'

'Yet you were sure that I was going to request a dance out of a sense of duty.' A pause, then, 'And if I was did it give you the right to refuse me?'

Around the glass her hands felt hot and sticky, her brain slightly woolly as he bent forward, much too near for her comfort. She saw the light on his black hair, the whiteness of his teeth.

'Only because a dance requested out of a sense of duty is never so enjoyable as one requested for pleasure,' she answered huskily.

'And you are sure the Duque de Valmardi never requested anything from the heart, not even a dance?'

Diane looked down into her wine, wishing that he was miles away. She decided on subterfuge.

'I suppose you could say that, like Maria, I'm now on the carpet?'

'On the carpet? I do not understand.'

'It's a saying we have, like being hauled before the head-mistress at school for some misdemeanour.'

He frowned and said stiltedly, 'You are under a misapprehension. I said nothing about you making an apology since you are of the opinion that I am to blame. Nevertheless, I find it distinctly puzzling as to why you should imagine that I dislike you. I might disapprove of your ways or your ideas, but I have never confessed to disliking you at any time.'

'Maybe you are too polite to admit it,' she said sweetly.

'One does not tell lies in order to be polite. However, since we are on the subject of Maria, I trust that you did not agree to her meeting that obnoxious man in the town yesterday?'

Diane looked him full in the eye. 'I was as surprised to see them together as you were. Or were you?'

He said with a dangerous quietness, 'I returned to the island sooner than I intended and I happened to see Arnaldo by the car, so I came in search of you. I then saw what appeared to be a prearranged meeting with you acting as chaperone. Now do you understand why I am eager for Maria to marry Felipe? He not only loves her, he is of an age to take care of her. Maria is not naughty, only a trifle foolish, with the foolishness of the inexperienced. There is nothing that time cannot put right. The right husband would prevent her making any more foolish mistakes. No doubt you will be acquainted with her little adventure— how she went to tea with a friend one day and on returning to the Quinta had to wait in the car half way home because the petrol had run out. Being Maria she could not wait, however, but set out to take a short cut home on foot. A storm came up and she was caught in it alone and lost. It was then that Pedro Banalda happened to come riding along on a horse and brought her home.'

Diane's face had lighted up. She said with a tender smile, 'I remember Maria writing to me about it. I thought it was so romantic.'

The temperature dropped with cataclysmic suddenness. The atmosphere was icy, but no less cold than the displeasure in his dark eyes. 'So you told her so, and you both dreamed your dreams. And you believe that you did not influence Maria after this—your own admission that you did just that?'

His eyes were black daggers which would willingly strike her through if it were possible, Diane was sure. She flinched beneath the heat of his anger, but she was no coward. Courage gave her a lift to her chin. The goblet of wine in her hands was forgotten.

'I know that I influenced her now,' she admitted. 'It was something she said that first evening at the Quinta. I never realised how much Maria had taken my letters to heart. I'm sorry—you were right.'

'You are aware that Maria magnified the incident out of all proportion. Her life was never in any danger from the storm and she was but five minutes from the Quinta when Banalda picked her up. But she was soaking wet and saw him as a knight errant. Unfortunately the man is a kind of Don Juan where the local *senhoritas* are concerned. Against my better judgment I gave him a post as chauffeur knowing that when Maria saw how he behaved with the *meninas* on my staff she would soon be disillusioned in the man. She was.'

'I wasn't particularly impressed with him myself,' Diane said, lowering her gaze down to the glass of wine before going on. Then, 'I do think that you've gone the wrong way about seeking her consent to marry Felipe, though. I would have said it would have been more polite for you to have been more casual about it, giving the impression that, in your opinion, she could do better elsewhere for a husband. You know,' she smiled up at him, her mouth sweetly curved, her eyes dancing, 'you can lead a horse to the drinking trough, but you can't make him drink. Let him go of his own accord and he'll soon be drinking to his heart's content.'

A gleam came into his dark eyes and was quickly gone. 'We will drink to that,' he said, striding across the room to pour himself a glass of the Madeira wine. Then he was back, lifting the glass, his dark eyes mocking hers over the rim. 'To Maria and Felipe, and to our friendship.'

Diane felt the wine going down her parched throat and chided herself for being a fool. Better to have him for an enemy than a friend. It would be like giving crumbs to a starving person. She would only end with wanting more. They were interrupted by a knock on the door. It was Bella.

'Alonso,' she cooed coquettishly, 'they are playing our tune. Shall we dance?'

Alonso frowned for a moment and listened to the rather evocative tune, muted through the closed door. Then he gave a slow smile and put down his glass.

'Why not?' he answered, and turned to Diane. 'You are returning to the dancing, of course?'

She let him take her glass and put it down beside his own on the table and they strolled out of the room together. Watching Alonso move away on to the dance floor with Bella in his arms, Diane knew that this was only the beginning to her torture at his indifference to herself.

At last the evening was over and Diane thanked Maria's mother sincerely for a wonderful party.

'I am so happy that you enjoyed it,' the older woman said, kissing her. 'It will only be one of many while you are here!'

Alone in her room later, Diane thought about Bella, who had never quite succeeded in concealing the hostility she felt towards herself. The worst of it was she was staying the night at the Quinta.

'I always find that going home after a wonderful party is rather a let-down, whereas if one stays on the party spirit lingers. Do you not agree?'

That appealing look from dark eyes had won the day for her. What more could a gracious hostess do than ask Bella to stay the night? Which was what Maria's mother did, despite signals to the contrary from her daughter.

'Really, it is too bad of Mother to ask Bella to stay the night,' she fumed. 'It is so blatantly done and it is not the first time she has wangled an invitation to stay. The trouble is that her visits usually go on for days.'

86

The two girls were going to their rooms later that same evening and had paused outside Diane's door.

Diane said carefully, 'Sometimes guests are not the kind one would choose to stay, but it's good manners to behave as though they were. Besides, have you ever considered trying to like Bella? After all, she could become your sister-in-law one day.'

Maria pressed her lips tightly together. Her small nostrils quivered.

'I could never like her no matter how I tried. Of course we always treat our guests with respect,' she said emphatically, 'but there are limits!' Suddenly she smiled and looked tenderly at Diane. 'Have you really enjoyed this evening? I know I have, despite Bella, and I know that you and I are going to have some good times together.'

Diane's answering smile was warm and tender. 'It has been wonderful,' she assured her, adding wistfully, 'You're lucky to have such a nice mother, Maria, a nice brother too, because they love you so much and wish only for your happiness.'

'I know,' Maria agreed. 'However, I shall not rise in time tomorrow for breakfast with Bella. I shall see you mid-morning for refreshment.'

Diane entered her room with mixed feelings, finding herself disliking Bella for the same reason as Maria because of her attachment to Alonso. In her heart a doubt had formed about the woman being the right wife for the Duque. He was of a reserved nature, and sometimes reserve hid deep feelings underneath, deep feelings that anyone who knew him could see that he was capable of. Diane's love for him was an unselfish one that wanted only the best for him to ensure a lifelong happiness. If Bella was planning to marry him for wealth and position then her feelings would come second, therefore they would be second-rate. He deserved better. But the choice was his and his alone. If marrying Bella would make him happy then she was all for it. Her own feelings did not matter. In a month maybe Diane McNair would be in London, looking back in a bittersweet way to her visit to Madeira.

Her sleep that night was dreamless and she awoke early to the sun streaming into her pretty room. The events of the previous evening came back gradually through the mists of sleep, and the presence of Bella in the Quinta was almost tangible. Diane lay for a while gazing up at the ceiling and wondering if Maria was awake. They could have arranged to go to the pool for an early morning swim and then gone out for the day and thus eluded Bella, but there could be other guests in the Quinta and Maria might be expected to stay indoors and entertain them. The last thing she wanted was to get Maria into trouble. However, there was no reason why she should not go for a swim herself. No one would be about yet, since it was only half past seven. No sooner had the thought occurred than Diane was out of bed and putting on her swimsuit. Then putting on her towelling robe and picking up a towel she stole quietly from the Quinta. Azaleas blazed with mimosa in the grounds and the heavy blossom of bougainvillaea was exotic. The birds were already singing in the trees and Diane wondered if they were looking on her kindly and not as an interloper. She hoped they were, for despite the beauty, luxury, and great wealth which the Quinta and grounds stood for it had been like home to her the last few days. The party the previous evening had been wonderful, the only discordant note being her love for Alonso. That was something she had to surmount and must use all her strength to do so.

There were no gardeners about when she rounded the wall of the plumbago to look towards the swimming pool. The next moment she stopped dead in her tracks, for someone was swimming lazily in the pool. The sun gleaming on the water glanced on the black head and the long brown arms cleaving through the water. Diane paled as she stared at him. The song of the birds, the perfume of flowers, the sun warm on her body receded into the background as she was aware of a strange frightening feeling of being alone with Alonso in a world in which he alone ruled. Her heart was beating so madly that her hand stole up to rest upon it.

Drawing back against the blossom, she waited until he left the pool, noticing the rippling muscles beneath a skin of deep tan like bronze satin as he moved with a long graceful stride to pick up his towelling robe and shrug into it. He would probably sit for a while on one of the loungers and smoke one of his favourite cheroots, she thought, and moved back behind the wall for a few moments before looking again. The pool had looked very tempting and she did not want to go back without her swim.

On the other hand she had no intention of meeting him. She was taking another peep around the corner of the plumbago when something loomed suddenly in front of her, cutting out the sun. There was a muttered exclamation as something solid cannoned into her and strong hands grabbed her painfully to keep her on her feet.

'What the . . .' Alonso exclaimed, and glared down into her startled face.

Diane stared up at him, too dismayed to do or say anything. Once again the surroundings had receded to a great distance as the grounds narrowed into proportions only big enough to contain Alonso and herself. It would have been more dignified to be able to move away from those long-fingered brown hands holding her so firmly, but it was a physical impossibility.

He had straightened from an unconscious frown of annoyance and an unreadable gleam lighted his eyes. Trust him to recover first, she told herself unhappily, as she slowly gathered her wits. As she recovered from the shock it was very difficult to remember to retain a certain degree of aloofness.

'I—I beg your pardon,' she stammered, her face like a rose. 'I—I never expected to—to meet anyone so early.'

'Which makes two of us,' he told her. Then he was smiling, his teeth a bar of whiteness in his tanned face. His eyes mocked the colour now flooding rosily from her slender throat to the edge of her hair line. 'I will warrant that Maria is not with you. I never expected to see either of you *senhoritas* up so early after the lateness of the hour you retired. You have half an hour before the gardeners arrive. Enjoy your swim.'

Diane was conscious of the sun shining on the strong waves the water had washed in his crisply curling hair and the pleasing angles of his clear-cut features. Then he was gone.

The water of the pool was deliciously cool and took her breath for a moment before it closed over her head. The next happy minutes in the water were pure bliss as she swam, floated on her back and swam again. Half an hour, Alonso had said, and she wondered if it had been an order. Her heart began to beat unsteadily again at the thought of him as a man magnificently built with the kind of bone structure of face and body calculated to devastate any feminine heart. The deep penetrating gaze of his had seemed to reach down into her very soul.

She had almost reached the wall of plumbago on her return to the Quinta when she came face to face with Bella. The slow smile revealing white teeth in a magnolia face carried a hint of insolence that was echoed in the dark eyes.

'So the early bird catches the worm, Miss McNair. Is that what you think?' she cooed. 'I saw you from my window making your way down to the pool and lying in wait for the Duque. It was well timed, that collision, was it not?'

Diane toyed with several cutting replies she could have made, but somehow it all seemed so pointless since she would be leaving the Quinta herself in the near future.

So she said, noting that Bella was fully dressed and had evidently come with the sole purpose of venting her jealousy and spite, 'Not only are your remarks uncalled-for, but I see the gardeners are arriving. Excuse me.'

She was trembling when she reached the room. A pity

that Bella could not hide her feelings instead of venting her spite on a guest at the Quinta, she thought unhappily. The woman simply could not spend her visit with dislike written all over her. It was unnerving to say the least. Diane leaned back against her door after closing it. And yet that same emotion tearing Bella apart could be likened to a similar emotion in herself. I'm as jealous of Bella as she is of me, she mused morosely, and she has more right to be jealous, since I'm the interloper. So I shall go to breakfast despite her.

The sun-dress she chose was a simple glazed cotton in fondant colours with a matching little top to change it into a day dress if needed. The skirt was full, flowing out from her slender waist and billowing out around long golden legs. She combed her silky hair into its usual natural style and slipped a heavy beaten gold bracelet on her arm.

To her surprise Alonso was on the terrace with his mother and Bella, about to begin breakfast. The sudden lifting of a dark brow at her appearance turned Diane's clear skin to rose. Her hesitation as she entered the sunny terrace was brief, for Alonso was already drawing a chair out for her at the table. She smiled at him, but found herself wishing that he had not been there. Bella was enough to confront on an empty stomach with their brief encounter in the garden still fresh in her mind, without Alonso.

As for Alonso, her so-called friendship with him was so fragile, so newly formed like a soap bubble that it would not take much to burst it. As yet Diane was not even certain about it. Fortunately his mother was there to greet her warmly and enquire if she had slept well. Bella said nothing. The dark eyes only came to life when she looked at Alonso. To his mother she was graciously polite. The meal passed smoothly with Alonso doing most of the talking and the others following his lead.

The morning air was soft and warm and filled with a golden translucent light with a sweet perfume rising from the flowers in the garden. To Diane, who sat facing the magnificent view, it was enough to gaze across the sparkling blue water and to feel the soft caress of the delicate morning breeze scarcely moving the palm trees. Her mouth curved tenderly at the sight and sound of the canaries gathered in the magnolia tree.

Alonso said lazily, 'Diane is enchanted with the canaries.'

His smile at her was openly mocking, a fact that Bella noted, for she was the one to answer.

'Our ways are so much different from Miss McNair's,' she ventured sweetly. 'She would never begin to understand us no matter how long she stayed. Do you not agree, *senhora*?'

Alonso's mother lifted finely penciled brows. 'I fail to see how I can agree,' she answered. 'I don't think I've fitted in so badly, do you, Alonso? After all, I was American when I married your father.'

Alonso's brilliant dark eyes rested fondly on his mother and he said something quick and teasing in Portuguese. Then he spoke in English.

'I think you forget, Bella,' he said lightly, 'that most of the industries which have made the island prosperous were started by the wonderful English.'

Wide-eyed and tense, Diane glanced at him swiftly and became instantly aware of glittering dark eyes and olive features that played havoc with her heart.

'Do I detect a note of censure, *senhor*?' she said coolly.

'Not at all,' he answered sardonically. 'I was merely stating a fact which is true nevertheless. We owe much to the British for making the economic structure of the island sound.'

'Really?' Diane looked at him levelly, forgetting for the moment the other occupants of the table. All her senses were centred on this aggravating, self-assured man who was so strong physically and mentally, and so ruthless in his power. Did she hear aright? Was he actually carrying a flag for her country? Her smile was demure. 'Perhaps you would enlighten me regarding these achievements of my countrymen?'

He inclined his dark head mockingly and made a negligent gesture to the golden wad of butter on the table.

'We can begin right here,' he said suavely. 'Butter was first made on this island by a British merchant in the year 1850. Now it is one of our chief exports. In the eighteen-forties a certain British major made the first sledge pulled by oxen for his invalid wife to ride in because she could not ride a horse. The wicker sledge made for the descent from Monté was also made by a member of a firm of wine shippers. A horticulturalist introduced pears, apples and strawberries here.' The dark eyes held her own captive as he went on. 'I could go on, of course, and mention the embroidery, rope-making and so on.'

'Thank you,' Diane said happily. 'You've made my day. I almost feel at home.'

'Almost?' he enquired mockingly. His smile was as un-expected as his conversation and Diane felt a kind of vibration near to her heart. 'We must leave it to Maria to make you feel a hundred per cent at home while you are here. By the way, where is Maria?'

The question was directed at his mother, who was evidently enjoying the conversation. With some amusement, she said, 'In bed.'

'But we have a visitor,' he said sternly. 'Maria should be at breakfast with our guests.'

His mother reached for a ripe peach from a dish of fruit and began to peel it. 'Come, Alonso,' she said lightly, 'I'm sure Diane is almost like one of the family and Bella is a distant relation. I can't see that Maria's presence is needed so urgently. After breakfast I planned on taking Diane to my room to see the embroidery work I've done. As for Bella, I'm sure you can look after her. I don't suppose Maria will be staying in bed all day.'

Alonso's eyes smouldered. 'I should hope not. Such a waste of a beautiful day,' he said tightly.

Diane felt a certain tension in the air and wondered if Alonso was vexed at his mother's frankness where Bella was concerned. He was angry over something. As for Bella, she sat there silent, a faint smile perpetually on her full lips, a smile that did not reach her eyes.

Diane felt almost light of heart and breathed in the

winelike air. She said, 'One of the pleasures of living in the hills is the scent of the pines. It's a kind of resinous smell that I find exhilarating.'

Alonso's mother chuckled. 'I believe the first seed was brought here by an Englishman,' she volunteered. 'But it was vine graftings from America that saved the wine crops here when they were destroyed by blight in the eighteen-seventies. Was that not so, Alonso?'

He agreed. 'That is so. The graftings were brought here by an Englishman, if the information is correct. Sorry, Mother.'

He grinned, then threw back his head to roar with laughter. Somehow it cleared the air for Diane and even the presence of Bella failed to dampen her spirits. Alonso had been on her side for once, as it were. It was idiotic to make an issue of it, but there it was.

Later when his mother showed her the beautiful embroidery on which she spent some of her time, Diane felt almost lighthearted.

'This is for you, Diane.'

The negligée that the Senhora de Valmardi gave to her was as delicate as butterflies' wings embroidered in pastel silk shades. Diane held her breath at the wonder of it.

'How beautiful!' she exclaimed, her eyes shining. 'It takes my breath away. I've never seen anything so fabulous. I simply don't know what to say. I shall have to keep it for my bottom drawer.'

The Senhora kissed her glowing face. 'You'll do no such thing. You will wear it. I shall do another set for your trousseau.'

Diane laughed derisively. 'My trousseau? But I haven't anyone in view at the moment.'

'You will have before very long. You're much too attractive to remain single for long.' The Senhora smiled sadly and walked to the window to gaze out at the view. 'I wish Alonso would marry. It's taking him so long to make up his mind and he's not the bachelor type. He is too much like his father.' Her sigh was a nostalgic one. 'He was a wonderful man, exciting, passionate, domineering and arrogant, but I loved him, for he was so kind and tolerant. We were very much in love.'

Diane replaced the negligée among the tissue paper. 'Maria thinks he will marry Bella,' she said. 'She is also of the opinion that he wants to see her married first before he takes the plunge himself.'

The Senhora shrugged slim shoulders. 'Alonso does give that impression, but one never really knows what he's thinking. He loves to tease, but he's strong-willed and will go his own way. As for Maria, there's only one man for her and that's Felipe.'

'You really think they will marry?'

'I'm sure of it, if only Alonso would give her time.' Again the Senhora sighed. 'However, it seems that Alonso has made up his mind whom to marry, because he has changed this last week or so. I've noticed him looking at his sister with exasperation. I would say that he's a man very much in love and impatient of the delay in announcing it.'

Diane drew in her lip and made an effort to speak lightly. 'I understand how you feel. I do hope everything turns out all right for you. I love Maria like a sister and my only wish is to see her happy.'

When Diane went to the terrace to take refreshment with Maria as arranged, the front door of the Quinta was opened and the long body of the Duque's gleaming car filled the aperture. The sun was shining on his dark hair as he helped Bella into the front seat. He was wearing immaculate mushroom-coloured slacks and a linen safari-style jacket in the neck of which was tucked a brown paisley scarf. He looked vital and charming, his smile startlingly white against the teak tan of his face as he said something to his companion which evidently pleased her.

It seemed to Diane, pausing momentarily in the hall, that the laugh, along with a surreptitious glance her way from the owner, held a note of triumph. Her thoughts were chaotic as she hurried on, too disturbed to hear her own name being spoken in the dimness of the hall. The next moment there was a detaining hand laid on her arm and she was looking up with a swift slightly hunted expression into Alonso's dark eyes.

With a narrowed look at her sudden delicate colour, he said, 'As I am taking Bella home I thought you would enjoy the drive with us. While it is not a very interesting trip in relation to the rest of the island, you will find it one of the least fatiguing. There is something I particularly want you to see, an enchanting old fountain with circular seats cut out in stone along with the names of people, mostly British.'

He had volunteered the last bit of information with a hint of satire, and Diane hesitated.

'It is not a long car run,' he went on. 'But first, a covering for your head.'

Just like that, she thought. He had commanded her presence like royalty and she was expected to accept.

'I'm sorry,' she said. 'I've arranged to have mid-morning refreshment with Maria.'

He gave a half smile, waving aside her excuse as though it was negligible. 'My little sister would be the last to wish to deprive you of an outing. We will leave her a message,' he said, and that was that.

Diane went up to her room for her shoulder bag and scarf, wondering how Bella was going to take her intrusion. Then remembering that she would only be with them on the outward journey, she picked up her shoulder bag and a nylon lace scarf to cover her hair.

The picot lace edging of the scarf framed her sweet face enchantingly as Alonso opened the door of the car and she slipped inside.

Bella had contrived not to meet her eyes, but she half turned towards the back seat to give Diane the benefit of her profile as she addressed Alonso.

'How very thoughtful of you, Alonso,' she cooed, 'to think of giving Miss McNair a little treat. It will be something for her to look back on when she has returned home.'

Her tone relegated Diane to that of a child being given a treat by a kind uncle, but she decided to ignore it. No point in coming out on a trip if one was to be niggled by little things which in the long run did not matter. The country they were passing through was mostly open moorland with interesting glimpses of workmen on the roads clad in thick brown wool caps, white heavy shirts and durable breeches. When they stood to one side to allow the car to pass they looked very fit and vibrant with health.

The land was cultivated and there were narrow ravines to cross amid terraced hills with the same degree of cultivation. Diane glimpsed a golf course as they swept on through Santo da Serra and soon they were in the little fishing town of Mechico. The car slid swiftly through the town taking a main road from which several smaller roads meandered into woods, and gradually they climbed into the hills.

The Vangroot residence was approached through tall iron gates opened by a woman in the black garb of a worker. Small thatched cottages led up to the imposing iron-gated entrance and they cruised along for quite a way before a second pair of double gates were opened on to the Quinta itself.

Alonso stopped the car at the porticoed entrance, helped Bella out and bent his dark head over her hand. The next moment he was back in the car. Sitting back in her seat, Diane felt anything but relaxed. His presence was like a series of tremors loaded with electricity. To strive for the careless attitude was something one had to do if one was to keep immune from his charms. Only when they had left the Vangroot residence far behind did she feel any measure of comfort.

He was driving slowly now and approaching the small town of Machico.

'It will no doubt surprise you,' he said conversationally, 'to know that in Machico it is possible to enjoy a cup of English tea. The tea rooms are always visited by English tourists who welcome a cup of their favourite brew after a long and dusty drive. I am sure that you will appreciate one.'

Diane borrowed some of his serenity. 'That is very kind of you to suggest it,' she said with her eyes on the back of his well-shaped dark head. 'I'd welcome a cup of tea.'

He parked the car outside the tea rooms and was round opening her door to help her out. Diane's legs felt a trifle shaky with the memory of the absent Bella, adding uneasiness to her other emotions. But the tea revived her, although any drink would have been welcome. They did not linger, for Alonso had places he wanted her to see before returning to the Quinta de Valmardi for lunch.

On returning to the car he put her into the front seat beside him. The road they were taking was lined with blue hydrangeas and a profusion of wild flowers. The woods, thick with eucalyptus and chestnut, added to the beauty of the landscape and mimosa stretched out unbroken as they neared Santo da Serra. The old fountain Alonso had mentioned earlier which he wanted her to see was at the end of stone steps below a bridge. While Alonso leaned against it Diane traced the names cut into the stone around the fountain with loving fingers.

He said sardonically, 'Since the names were carved at the beginning of the eighteenth century they can have little or no meaning now. Most of them, I would say, are the names of sailors and adventurers who landed here a century ago.'

Diane nodded. 'I know, but it does give me a warm feeling to know that some were British.'

On the way back Alonso slowed the car to point out areas of smallholdings where the poorer people dwelt in thatched cabins and half-timbered walls instead of the colour-washed walls and shuttered windows of the rich. Most of them had their meals outdoors, against the colourful landscapes of begonias, geraniums, passion flowers, huge dahlias, bougainvillaea and hydrangeas. To Diane it was a scene from another world where woodcutters still carried their bundles of wood home and people lived in fairytale surroundings untouched by modern civilisation.

As he talked Alonso glanced at her from time to time, his

eyes narrowing on her excited face as she cried out in admiration or amusement at some little incident which caught her attention. Her low laugh of pleasure was, like her chuckle, unintentionally provocative. Until now, Diane had checked her words, her glances, even her thoughts in his presence at moments when she had wanted to be herself, although common sense had counselled otherwise. But with all the strange beauty of another world opening before her eyes she had momentarily forgotten his existence. The woodcutters labouring home beneath their burdens, the gay gathering of families in their gardens for lunch, the almost medieval dwellings looking like fairytale encampments amid the profusion of tropical growth had taken her breath away.

Gradually as the car cruised very slowly along the roads, Alonso's glances towards her became more prolonged. He had never before sensed this curious freshness of an English girl, a quality of delicate fragrance which had to be experienced to be believed. It had to be congenital, coming neither from scent nor artifice but from herself. Once during a sudden silence between them Diane's eyes had met his with a little tingling shock which startled her even though it was gone in a flash.

She said to hide her embarrassment, 'I suppose you think I'm a romantic, but I can't help but be so since I've come to the island. I've been trying to remember the legend of Machico.' She laughed, a tinkling little sound that brought a smile to his well cut mouth.

'Then I had better tell it to you,' he answered.

'Would you?' She sounded so surprised that he raised a dark brow. 'Wasn't it to do with two lovers eloping?'

'That is so,' he agreed mildly. 'The story goes that a certain Robert Machim, a subject of Edward III, fell in love with a maiden named Ana d'Arfet. Unfortunately Ana's parents did not look upon him with favour since he was not of noble birth like their daughter, so they forbade him to see her again. Needless to say the couple eloped from Bristol in a ship to Brittany, but they were caught in a storm and swept south to the bay where Machico now stands. Going ashore, they rested beneath a cedar tree, but the journey had been too much for poor Ana, who finally succumbed in her lover's arms. Robert buried her beneath the cedar tree and died soon after from a broken heart. A chapel was built on the spot where the cedar tree once stood.'

'And Machico, which is Portuguese, was named after him,' Diane said. 'Thank you for a very enjoyable outing.'

His dark eyes narrowed at her enigmatically. 'One learns something from every journey, be it short or long,' he remarked, putting on speed and glancing at his watch.

Her look his way was clear-eyed and curious. 'Don't tell me that you learned something too?'

'Why not? One is never too old to learn. Like you, I learn fast,' he said with a hint of satire.

'Do I learn fast?' she asked breathlessly. 'If I do I wasn't aware of it.'

'Intelligent people never are,' was the cool reply.

'Oh, thank you,' Diane murmured, with a feeling that they were on dangerous ground. Perhaps it was as well that they were fast approaching the Quinta. It had certainly been an enlightening morning.

CHAPTER SIX

DIANE was sure there was no more accommodating place than Madeira. The town was a delight to wander around, with the shopkeepers anxious to sell their wares with the satisfaction of the customers in mind. One had only to hesitate on choosing a certain blouse or dress and at least half a dozen would be dispatched to the Quinta to ponder over. Although flowers grew in abundance at the Quinta Diane could never resist purchasing a bunch each time she was in town from the pretty flower-sellers in their red embroidered skirts, white blouses and red boleros. She would return to the Quinta with her arms filled with flowers, to the amusement of the Senhora and Maria.

Once on her return to the Quinta she had met Alonso, who raised a silky black brow at the sight of his English guest, lovely hair windblown, cheeks glowing and eyes clear and shining, with a bunch of beautifully arranged blooms in her arms.

'Do we not have enough flowers at the Quinta?' he remarked sardonically. 'Or is your desire for them insatiable?'

His dark eyes had narrowed on the charming picture she had made and Diane felt idiotically happy. She had felt like taking one and putting it in his buttonhole, but one did not do such things to the Duque de Valmardi.

'I simply can't resist them,' she had answered demurely. 'They are so beautiful, and the girls who sell them are like flowers themselves. You have a very beautiful island here, Alonso.'

His name slipped out easily these days, but she always felt a tremor near her heart whenever he used her name. Since the outing to Machico she had not seen him very often. He was out most days around the estate and they did not always meet at meals. Some evenings he dined out.

101

On one memorable evening he had taken the three women to Funchal to see a select cabaret at one of the leading night spots, but it seemed to Diane that he kept his distance. There was a tantalising aloofness in him that Diane found fascinating. It heightened his magnetism, his nonchalant way of walking while holding his shoulders erect and square and the perfection of his tanned features.

His immaculate appearance came from being in a place where time ceased to exist. There was an aura about the place, giving one limitless time to give attention to detail, the latter being essential to good grooming. But well groomed or otherwise, Alonso could never fail to arouse a woman's interest and hold it—Diane was sure of that. Maybe it was the Latin in him carrying him forth with an efficient nonchalance that impressed her so deeply.

If Diane had ever fancied herself in love with anyone before it had been a travesty, a pale insignificant shadow beside the love she felt for Alonso. And the trouble was that she had so much time now to think about him. As she woke up leisurely in the morning, or relaxed in a perfumed bath, his image would materialise to taunt her, shutting out all other thought. She avoided him as much as possible. Caught between shame, bewilderment and anger, she despised herself for falling beneath his spell. The days slipped by to the haunting music of sweet sounds in glorious sunshine. Breakfast on the terrace was a cup of nectar to be drained to the last delicious drop. Around half past ten both girls sauntered down to the swimming pool, sometimes in a mist-like vapour which habitually surrounded the hills in the mornings. It was, however, warm and friendly, gradually disintegrating as the sun came out in full force. Then, in the heat of the sun, they would find morning activities were sufficient and after lunch would retire to their rooms to rest. But whatever Diane did was performed with the maximum amount of pleasure and she adored the exquisite beauty of the warm velvet nights. They represented the end of a perfect day.

Then it became a world such as fairy tales are made of,

shutting out all material things that had a way of intruding into dreams. From her balcony Diane loved to watch the startling sudden change from day into night with a hesitant glimpse of twilight in between. First came the sudden hush and gradually the springing into life of strings of lights garlanding the bay. Then the clusters of lights against the backcloth of the hills sparkling like jewels, and the blissful quietening of the heart as one became enveloped in a sense of stillness and peace. Later she would stroll in the gardens before retiring with the golden effulgence of lights among the trees turning everywhere into a fairy bower.

One memorable evening she had come across Alonso smoking his last cheroot before bed. Her heart had leapt at the sight of his tall frame with his wide shoulders outlined against the dimness. With a sigh coming from deep inside her, Diane knew that pleasing though the cigar aroma was, any future encounter with that same aroma would bring bittersweet memories of a man who had stormed her heart and taken it for all time, who could never be hers.

'Good evening, Alonso,' she said as calmly as she could.

He looked down at her with a vague interest that piqued her pride. She had a notion that he regarded her as a second Maria and it irritated. He inclined his dark head politely.

'Diane—what brings you out into the garden so late? Did you enjoy your day?'

'Very much,' she replied.

She watched him throw the fragments of his cigar on to the ground and grind it out with his heel. Then she swiftly lowered her face from his searching look. It was a movement of self-preservation against those dark eyes that saw far too much. Her love for him had deepened in intensity, encouraged unconsciously in a beautiful world where one could dream dreams. Her feelings for him now were too near to the surface of self-control. Only pride and the feeling of being a fool helped her to keep her love secret. That and the knowledge that if she turned away and left him he would not even notice that she had gone. By staying on she could be like Bella, outstaying her welcome where he was concerned. There was another aspect too, a fear of an eventual break-through of a longing and pent-up agonised need which only he could satisfy.

Her foolish imagination worked overtime, imagining him coming eagerly towards her in the manner of lovers meeting, his hands held out and thrusting through her hair, hauling her against him roughly and making passionate love. His deep voice vibrating on the night air jerked her back to reality.

He said evenly, his dark eyes fixing her face in the gloom, 'Not feeling homesick yet for the bright lights and the freedom you have left behind? Many of our young people become too restless to enjoy the solitude and peace of the island. To those who come here it is an unknown quantity which once savoured is not of their choosing. Perhaps the tranquillity and peace is not for you?'

Diane thought hollowly that he was right. Tranquillity and peace were not for her while she remained living under his roof, seeing him continually with Bella, even to being invited to their wedding. A cold shiver ran through her at the thought, and instantly his hand on her arm was warm and vibrant.

'You are cold? Come, we must go indoors. We must not risk you catching a chill, for we have planned an interesting weekend for you.'

He was guiding her towards the Quinta as he talked and Diane shot him a clear-eyed glance. 'For me?' she queried curiously.

'For you. We are going to pay a visit to Maria's intended, Felipe,' he answered suavely. He gave a half smile. 'You see, I do regard him as my future brother-in-law, despite my little sister's obstinacy.'

With a feeling that the subject was one she would rather not discuss, Diane moved forward quickly and entered the Quinta. He still had his hand on her arm; a pulse was beating madly in her throat, and she knew without a shadow of doubt that he was hopelessly and obsessively in her blood. Confused and bewildered by the depth of her feelings, feelings which she regarded as being alien to her, Diane dragged herself back to the import of what he was saying. 'You are pleased about the visit?'

'Yes.' The sound of her own voice, cool and even, gave her courage. 'Since it means another journey through the lovely countryside and a visit at the end of it.'

'So you are pleased to leave the Quinta de Valmardi? Are you not happy here?'

'Of course, but it is nice to know that I am seeing as much of the island as possible during my stay. Everything is so overwhelmingly beautiful and the gorgeous sun is cooking me to a ripe tan.' She smiled up at him in the dimness, her clear eyes bright, perhaps with a suggestion of tears behind. Strange and heartbreaking, she thought, that he was quite unmoved by her presence when his was making her tingle from top to toe. 'You are being very kind to someone whose presence does not please you.'

'You please Maria,' he answered after a brief pause, his eyes narrowing down on the peach-like bloom of her face, the shining eyes and the aura of bright hair gleaming softly in the subdued lighting among the trees. 'When do you plan to leave?'

The last few words hit her with cataclysmic suddenness She swallowed on a dry throat, and shuddered, recoiling from a mortal blow. So he could not wait to be rid of her. Hastily, she lowered her head and steadied her bottom lip between her teeth. It took quite an effort to appear casual.

'I haven't made any plans yet,' she said in a voice which sounded remarkably steady above the tumult inside her. 'In any case, I don't intend to outstay my welcome.'

'You were invited to stay,' he reminded her coolly. 'We shall be pleased for you to stay as long as you wish.'

'Thank you.'

Her answer was barely audible as she flitted away in the direction of her room, not giving him time to say more. Her first reaction on reaching her room was to pack and leave the next morning. Then second thoughts took over, urging her to be sensible and think of Maria, who would be very distressed at her leaving so suddenly.

As she prepared for bed Diane recalled Alonso's voice, dark with meaning when he had told her of the forthcoming visit to Felipe. He expected her to concentrate on the situation between his sister and Felipe perhaps to do all in her power to influence Maria into accepting her suitor should he propose. But she rebelled against the prospect, seeing it was Maria's own business and nobody else's. And there was her own reaction to the presence of Alonso, for he was sure to accompany them. He had said that she was welcome to stay with his usual lugubrious authority. She was an idiot to be so hypersensitive about the man. His polite indifference to herself was a masterpiece of insensitivity and she must be mad to be in love with such a man.

But she fell asleep haunted by strange fears and in her restless turnings saw Maria eloping with a man on a horse through a swirling mist. Then Alonso was bearing down on her, also on a horse, his face tense with anger.

'It is all your fault,' he called out. 'You have spoiled everything. I will deal with you later!'

Diane awoke to tears on her cheeks and slept fitfully for the rest of the night, to awake in the morning with the sun melting away all her restless dreams.

'We are going to Felipe's *quinta* on Saturday. So we had better go to the town before then to buy anything extra that we might need.'

Maria lay beside Diane at the swimming pool on a lounger. Her long, beautifully manicured fingers were raking absently through the silk-wet strands of her hair as it dried in the sun.

Diane said carefully, 'Haven't you just come from there? Will you mind going again so soon?'

Maria's face, devoid of any make-up, looked extraordinarily childish in the golden sunlight. She yawned prettily and Diane had to fight against echoing it, feeling drained and empty from lack of sound sleep and the problem of Alonso. There were so many things she wanted to ask.

'I do not mind.' Maria sounded too casual for Diane's peace of mind. 'Felipe's aunt is rather strict, but she is nice. You will like her. Felipe has her as chaperone until he marries. The Quinta is Felipe's, given to him by his parents. He has done much to expand the farm and wine-making. Alonso is talking about going into partnership with him with the wine.'

'So it would be just perfect for you to marry Felipe,' Diane said thoughtfully. 'Are his parents well off?'

'Extremely, but there are four sons and Felipe is the second son. I wonder if he will invite any of his brothers to come to meet you at the Quinta. They are not as handsome as he is and the eldest is married. He lives in Aporto.'

Diane only half listened to what her friend was saying. She was more concerned about Alonso and about his constant presence during the visit to Felipe's *quinta*. To her dismay Bella came to dinner that evening. Her first intimation of the impending visit came from the Senhora. They were going towards the *sala* that evening together. Maria had pleaded a headache and was staying in her room. The Senhora said that Maria had these attacks of migraine from time to time, when she preferred to be alone and rest until she was well again. The strange thing was that they had only begun during the past two years. Diane thought that it was quite possible that the attacks had been brought on because of her brother's continued friendship with Bella, whom Maria could not stand. The attack tonight could be accounted for by the fact that Bella would be present at dinner.

They were going down the staircase to the hall when the Senhora said,

'Bella has some business with Alonso which they're to discuss this evening, so I invited her to dinner. I believe she's arriving right now.'

Alonso was striding across the hall below as she spoke. The footman was opening the door and Bella entered.

Diane thought that tonight she looked striking but plain. Her rather sallow features, viewed from a distance, had a kind of hardness about them and only her dark eyes provided colour. Her dark hair was strained back from her face, accentuating the hard lines, but her dress was richly embroidered and her jewels were certainly not paste even to Diane's inexperienced eye. She was a woman who demanded attention and who was certainly getting it from Alonso, who bent his dark head over her hand to greet her charmingly.

The next moment she was staring at the two women descending the staircase and the Senhora went graciously to meet her. Diane followed more slowly, inclining her head and borrowing some of Bella's coolness when they met. In the *sala* Diane was careful to choose a chair opposite to the chaise-longue which the Senhora usually occupied, leaving Bella to sit beside her hostess. Alonso served wine and in order to avoid contact with his fingers, Diane took her glass from him far too quickly. It tilted and some of the wine spilled down on to her dress.

Instantly Alonso was full of apologies, whisking a crisp white handkerchief from his pocket to soak up the wine.

Diane said in some confusion, 'It was my fault for being so clumsy.' It occurred to her then that he might guess the reason for the accident, simply that his close proximity embarrassed her. This is awful, she thought, going cold inside to see Bella's eyes boring into her across the room. The woman would come to the same obvious conclusion, that she was in love with Alonso. Diane knew that she was only pretending to listen to what the Senhora was saying, that her thoughts were all centred across the room to Alonso and herself. Her smile, though enigmatic, was secret and knowing. Diane shared Maria's dislike of the woman intensely in that moment and found herself envying that young woman's migraine which kept her upstairs.

But the evening had to be got through. Fortunately the wine spilled on her dress was negligible. All the same it was a relief to excuse herself to go and sponge the stain out.

The Senhora followed her upstairs, very concerned. 'Your lovely dress!' she exclaimed in sympathetic tones. 'I was admiring it and Bella agreed that it was very becoming.'

Diane, glancing up at the sweet face of her hostess as she sponged the offending mark, thought, the poor dear hasn't the slightest inkling that Bella is jealous of me. The smile she gave her covered an unhappiness mixed with anger at herself for being such an idiot. She was tempted to excuse herself from going down to the *sala* again on the pretext of a headache or something. She was in no mood for a dinner arranged for Bella and Alonso. But it would be churlish to refuse to accompany the Senhora back again to the *sala*. It did occur to her on their way downstairs that the older woman had acted discreetly in leaving Alonso and Bella together. But it would only be a forerunner of many more meetings between them and she had to face them with fortitude until her visit was over.

The meal ended eventually and after coffee Alonso went to his study with Bella, leaving the two women alone. They listened to music on records and the Senhora picked up her latest piece of embroidery, some negligée for Maria. Diane looked at the fragile exquisite silk and knew that Maria's mother was as anxious as her son for her daughter to marry the absent Felipe and to have grandchildren around her. The Senhora's smile was sweet.

She said dreamily, 'The first time I saw Madeira I was captivated by its beauty. I arrived in the spring and Funchal was breathtaking, with the avenues of coral trees a fiery red against the blue of the sky and the enchanting blossom of jacarandas. Then I came to the Quinta de Valmardi, and if I had thought that Funchal had resembled a garden its beauty was nothing to the grounds here. Even so, I discovered other *quintas* with fabulous gardens too, as you will no doubt see. They were created by Portuguese noblemen who settled here and proceeded to make an Eden of their surroundings. Many of them, like the Quinta here, have vast parklands in the old aristocratic traditions of long ago.' She chuckled softly. 'Alonso is very much

Portuguese in tradition, despite his English and American education. You'll have perhaps noticed that?'

'He's very Latin-looking and—handsome,' Diane admitted reluctantly, not enjoying the turn in the conversation. 'And Maria is very pretty too.'

'But Maria hasn't Alonso's strength of character. Of course, one can't expect it. My son is so very masculine and arrogant, whereas Maria is perhaps too easily led. I sometimes wish that she had some of Alonso's strength of will.'

'In which case I would say you would certainly have had problems with your daughter,' Diane said demurely. 'She could easily have taken it into her head to remain single for as long as your son, which would be a tragedy as far as she's concerned. Maria was meant for marriage and children. She'll make an ideal mother, being sweet and kind and also sincere in her emotions.'

'And don't you want to be married, Diane? I would say the same about you as regards being meant for marriage. Perhaps we can fix you up with someone here. Maria would be thrilled to have you near for always and so shall I. We've grown very fond of you.'

But not Alonso, Diane thought unhappily. For ecstatic moments she allowed her dreams full rein and imagined being married to Alonso, having his children, a small arrogant strutting boy, lovably dark and handsome, and a small girl whom he would adore. But it was not for her, this dream of not only having a husband but a sister whom she adored too.

'You're very sweet, *senhora*,' she answered, coming back to reality. 'Of course I would like to marry, but I want to fall in love first. No doubt you'll think that's sentimental. But it's the way I am.'

'And rightly so. I was very much in love with my husband. I couldn't have left everything I held dear, my home, parents, relations and friends otherwise.' The Senhora broke off a thread with her white even teeth and leaned forward to pat Diane's hand. 'Not to worry, the right man will come along when he's ready.'

She chuckled as Alonso entered the *sala* with Bella at that moment.

'What is the joke?' he asked. 'Can we share it?'

The Senhora shook her head. 'I'm afraid not. There was no joke to be shared,' she replied lightly. 'I trust you two have completed your business?'

'We have.' Alonso was noncommittal. With a pleasant shrug of wide shoulders he seated Bella, then went to pour out wine. He was suave and smiling as if well pleased with events of the evening. There had been a softness in his tone as he addressed his mother and a marked gentleness as he had seated Bella. The incident of the spilled wine earlier in the evening came back in force and Diane noticed that he was pouring wine for all three of them. Not again, she thought. Once in an evening is enough. The sparkling Madeira wine took on the guise of the horrible mixture he had given to her when she had Madeira fever.

Suddenly she was on her feet. 'No wine for me, thanks. I find it as strong as the Madeira air, and I'm rather tired. So if you'll excuse me.'

Diane hoped that her small laugh sounded natural. It was the best she could do with all three faces turned her way in polite surprise. But she was past caring. She flitted across the room hoping to outwit Alonso's long stride, only to find him at the door to open it politely.

Diane murmured something, did not wait for his reply, and went swiftly from the room. On the way up the staircase she tried not to care that Alonso's life had nothing to do with her, and that Bella knew far more about him than she would ever know. A link was forged between them, a link that had existed long before she had met him. No matter what she did or said nothing could alter that. Her nerves felt tense. Fond though she was of Maria, she would give anything in that moment never to have written to her at all.

Maria was asleep when she called in to see how she was before going to her room. She lay there sleeping as blissfully as a child. True, she had the naïveté of one who had led a sheltered life with a sublime unawareness of the world

111

and all its problems, and an infallible belief that everything would come right if she willed it. But wasn't that how Alonso behaved too? Not that one could ever accuse him of being naïve even as a child. He had been far too intelligent —of that Diane was sure.

To fall in love with Alonso had probably been the unhappy lot of quite a few women who had known him, and she was proving just as vulnerable as the rest. The terrible thing was that there was no cure for it. And how could she argue that Bella's love for him was less than her own, more selfish?

The car was climbing steadily upwards and Diane had the strange feeling that they were climbing to the top of the world. Scarves of mist wrapped themselves around the mountain peaks as though caught on the jagged edges against their will and the road was now narrow and twisting alarmingly high above an abyss. There was a sheer drop on one side into sheer nothingness, and Diane marvelled at Alonso's coolness as he handled the big car smoothly around hazardous bends. He might have been driving in the heart of the city, for he was so calm and casual as he talked to his mother seated beside him.

Diane could not look at the back of that dark well-shaped head without a small knot of pain in her throat. It gave her a bittersweet feeling of having him to herself away from Bella. For the moment he was free again and she could live in hope of his closeness becoming bearable.

She glanced at Maria sharing the back seat of the car with her and wondered what this visit would entail. Would she change her mind and accept Felipe? In any case Diane would not interfere. The mist was clearing now and they were turning inland to cruise between sugar cane, vineyards and banana plantations.

'Felipe's estate,' Maria said laconically. 'Soon you will see the Quinta.'

Along a road lined with fiery red coral trees contrasting colourfully against a blue sky Diane suddenly realised that the mist had gone and that they were now approaching an imposing villa, simply but picturesquely designed. Within minutes Alonso was pulling up smoothly at the imposing portico where Felipe awaited them. His tall frame dwarfed the diminutive one of the woman beside him.

'Welcome to the Quinta.' Felipe was smiling broadly as he greeted Alonso before bending courteously over the Senhora's hand. 'My aunt cannot wait to meet you, Miss McNair,' he said to Diane after reluctantly tearing his eyes away from Maria, who had refused to meet his ardent gaze. 'My aunt, Senhora Luisa Gardeiro.'

The small woman beside him, in black offset by delicate white lace at wrists and throat, came forward to greet her courteously with a look of unmistakable pleasure lighting up her dark eyes.

'I am very pleased to meet you, Miss McNair,' she said quietly in English. Her accent spoke of a language that was foreign to her, but there was no doubt of the warmth of her greeting. 'Maria has told me so much about you that I feel I know you.'

'Precisely what I think,' Alonso's mother put in warmly with a smile at Diane. 'Indeed, Diane is like one of the family.'

'Miss McNair is a remarkable young woman. Maria is very attached to her.' Alonso had moved up beside Diane as he spoke and she glanced up swiftly at his sardonic expression. 'One learns something every moment from the incredible English.' His smile was openly mocking and Diane stiffened inwardly.

Sarcastic brute! she thought angrily, and longed to hit him. However, the moment passed and they all moved leisurely across the hall to ascend the beautifully carved staircase. The *sala* they entered was filled with the pleasing aroma of burning logs from the white marble fireplace where the flames crackled merrily. The glow from it highlighted the rich brocade window drapes, the exquisitely carved furniture and the silver on the tea tray awaiting the guests. Flowers were arranged as though to meet the eyes whichever way they turned and their fragrance was pleasing.

When the women were seated Felipe and Alonso left them to their refreshment. The Senhora's small beringed hands served tea from a silver pot and small cakes were handed around with eggshell cups of steaming liquid.

Maria, graceful and demure in her beautifully simple dress of soft mushroom silk, gave Diane a teasing look of reassurance. The *sala* presented a perfect setting for her. She had the air of belonging and Diane was not surprised that Felipe loved her so much. With her soft brown eyes and creamy magnolia skin framed by black silky hair, she was indeed enchanting. The utter sweetness of her expression spoke of a tranquillity which came from deep down within. At the moment, though, there was something indomitable about the small firm chin tilted to reveal the long lovely line of her throat.

The thought brushed Diane's mind at that moment that Maria would marry Felipe soon enough when Alonso had married. She was holding off only because she did not want him to marry Bella. Poor Maria, how disappointed she must have been when I wouldn't entertain the idea of interfering between her brother and Bella, Diane thought wretchedly. It was not a very happy note on which to begin what otherwise could have been an enjoyable visit.

In a graciously furnished suite, Diane had a bath and changed into a soft beige jersey dress. She was ready when Maria knocked on her door, gave her arm a reassuring squeeze and promptly escorted her downstairs.

Felipe and Alonso were in the hall below looking very handsome in evening dress. It occurred to Diane that the two men got on together as well as Maria and herself. And no wonder, for Alonso had that congenital charm which worked with either sex. Strange that he should cover up a hard inaccessible interior with so much charm. Strange also that he should remain a bachelor for so long when there were so many beautiful women strewn around like flowers in his path. He had been of a marriageable age when Maria was little more than a girl. Why then had he not married years ago? Upon this thought they had reached the hall, and Diane resolutely decided to forget the Duque and concentrate upon her host, Felipe.

Indirectly this resolve carried her a little into the enemy camp with Alonso. Nothing escaped that dark gaze and the sight during the meal of Felipe sitting with his head inclined in Diane's direction on his right hand at the table most of the time no doubt interested him profoundly. Several times she felt that intent gaze travelling over the crystal glass and flower arrangements along the table from where he sat to rest thoughtfully on her.

To be quite truthful, Diane had been so interested in Felipe's conversation that she had been oblivious to Alonso seated further down the table. Felipe's mother was English and she had met her husband while on holiday in Portugal. It had been love at first sight for the English girl on her first holiday abroad and for the Portuguese nobleman. They had been very happy in their union, and Felipe loved to talk about his pretty English mother and the happiness she had brought to them as a family.

'You will meet her later, for she is coming towards the end of the year to spend some time with me here,' he told Diane enthusiastically. Then he added regretfully, 'I was hoping to be celebrating my own marriage by then.'

Maria was chatting with the Senhora Luisa on her other side when he confided the last bit of information.

Diane murmured, 'You mean to Maria? Maybe you're not going about it in the right way. Don't appear too eager. Pay attentions to another woman, make her jealous.'

Felipe was aghast at the suggestion. 'I could not possibly do that. It would mean the other woman losing face in our society. Besides, how could I be sure that she would not use the situation to her own advantage and force me into marrying her?'

'I see what you mean,' Diane answered mildly, forgetting for the moment how strict the Portuguese were about their womenfolk where men were concerned. Suddenly she smiled. 'You could try me. I would be safe enough.'

Felipe laughed. 'You are joking, are you not?'

'No, I'm perfectly serious. I must be, since I've been convincing myself that it was wrong to interfere in other people's lives and that nothing would induce me to do it. Now I'm doing just that, but only because I'm convinced that Maria is fond of you and that she's stubbornly refusing to marry you until Alonso has settled down himself with a wife.'

'Ah, why did not I think of that?' Felipe said soberly. 'So you think that the love of my life really does love me in return and that Alonso is between us?'

Diane began to get alarmed. 'Goodness, Felipe, you'll have me shot if Alonso hears of this! He's not between you and Maria. Maria is regarding him in that light.'

Their voices had been lowered to confidence level and consequently their heads, the fair one and the red-gold one, were very close together. In questioning the wisdom of speaking to Felipe as she had done about Maria, Diane's eyes were drawn down the length of the table to see that Alonso was looking at her. She looked quickly away again, knowing that she was not behaving in a way that Alonso would approve. From where he sat it could appear as if she and Felipe were already on intimate terms. No doubt if he was making a comparison with the women of his world the English Miss was certainly living up to his unflattering opinion of her. Well, let him! she thought furiously.

Felipe's glance at her was quizzical. 'I understand that you do not wish me to say anything of this to Alonso. But I assure you that he is my very good friend. He is coming into partnership with me in the wine business and he has done much to help me make the estate a paying proposition. He has also helped me in the irrigation of the land, a problem forever with anyone who resides on a volcanic island.'

Hastily, Diane said, 'That's all very well, but I know he wouldn't approve of you and me playing a part in bringing Maria closer to you. If I weren't so sure about it I wouldn't mention it at all. But it must be a secret between you me.'

She shrugged slim shoulders philosophically. 'We only need to impress Maria with an interest in each other, then we can watch what happens.'

'The more I consider it the more I see the endless possibilities of such a suggestion. I kiss your hand. You are indeed my friend.'

'You're catching on quickly,' Diane said as Felipe suited the action to the word. 'One thing, though—we must be discreet when Alonso is about. Please remember we're doing this for Maria.'

'And for me,' Felipe ended firmly. 'I shall not forget your kindness.'

'Don't be too premature with your thanks,' she whispered urgently. 'I only hope things go the way we want them to, that's all.'

'What were you and Felipe talking about so urgently at dinner?' Maria asked later when, leaving the two men to smoke their cheroots, she and Diane followed the two older women to be main *sala* for coffee and liqueurs. 'You were very engrossed. And what did he kiss your hand for?'

Diane slanted a glance at Maria's pouting profile and congratulated herself on her perception. Was it possible for Maria to be jealous?

'Don't forget,' she said, 'that Felipe's mother is English.'

'And what is that supposed to mean?'

'Only that Felipe feels a kind of bond between the English and his father's people which is only natural in the circumstances. So he was just being polite and making me feel very welcome in his *quinta*.' She peered sideways into Maria's charming face. 'You aren't jealous, are you?'

Maria's reaction to this was a swift denial, but it was not accompanied by her usual humour.

'Of course I am not. Jealous of Felipe? I could never be jealous of Felipe being nice to my friend. I am annoyed, Diane, that you should regard me as being capable of such a thing.'

'Then don't look such a crosspatch.' Diane's voice was teasing.

Maria wrinkled a creamy brow. 'Crosspatch?' she echoed. 'I do not understand.'

'It means that you're looking extremely annoyed,' Diane explained, and laughed.

Maria was very subdued for the rest of the evening and even when the two men appeared she remained the same. True, Felipe asked Diane if she would like to see over the Quinta and she accepted with alacrity and left the room with him, completely oblivious of Maria watching them go. She quite enjoyed the tour of the rooms, making a laughing suggestion here and there when they came to suites of rooms suitable perhaps for a nursery or playrooms.

But if Maria had become suddenly moody Felipe was in top form. He was happy and relaxed with his English guest and Diane responded to his easygoing charm. Maria was the first to retire when they were all assembled once more in the *sala*.

Diane looked anxiously at her set little face. 'Oh, Maria, not another of your migraine attacks?' she asked sympathetically. She had followed the girl to the door of the *sala* to put the question in a low voice. 'I'm sorry,' she added with feeling.

Maria said primly, 'It will soon pass. I will see you in the morning. *Boa noite*, Diane.'

Diane walked with her to the foot of the stairs, then made her way towards the front door feeling in need of air. Suppose the game she was playing with Felipe had really upset her little friend? She went cold inside. What a worry her visit to Madeira was turning out to be!

The last thing she wanted was to cause any kind of distress to her very dear friend Maria. What to do now? Tell Felipe to forget the whole thing? But wasn't that defeating their sole purpose? Wasn't she getting into a tizzy because Maria was reacting so splendidly to the little scheme? Diane strolled outdoors in the perfumed air of the garden. One way or another it had been quite an evening. The two *senhoras* evidently had much in common, with embroidery being one of their favourite subjects. It was one that no visitor to the island could get away from in any case, since the women and girls who carried on the craft on the island were to be seen in every street and at most of the cottage windows.

While Maria admired it she did not seem to be taken up with it the same as the older women, who did it for a hobby. And Alonso, she noticed, always made himself scarce when the subject came up in his hearing. Here she was again, thinking of Alonso, and not five minutes out of his presence! He was much too close to her heart; too magnetic to her senses. Diane found no pleasure tonight in the well planned grounds with the flowers and blossoms looking wax-like and perfect in their lovely setting. And it seemed stupid to come out at all when she really was tired and wanting her bed.

'Miss McNair, so here you are. I thought that you had retired with Maria. Is she all right? I thought she looked pale, worried,' Felipe said anxiously.

Diane patted his arm reassuringly. 'Don't worry. I hardly like to put it down to our little plan working out so soon, but there it is. You know, Felipe,' a little sad smile hovered about her sweetly curved mouth, 'I'm all kinds of a heel to be doing this to my own sex, betraying Maria, as it were. I only hope it will lead to her ultimate happiness.'

They had strolled along one of the many paths between a profusion of flowers looking strangely wax-like in the gloom. To Diane the very air was poignant with tears.

'It just has to,' Felipe said firmly. 'I shall never marry anyone else if I cannot have Maria. She is my life.'

Diane smiled up at him, at the golden hair a light cap in the faded light, the eyes dark with longing between fair lashes, and she felt very much alone at that moment.

'You're a very nice person, Felipe,' she said with a sweet smile. 'You and Maria are two of the nicest people I've ever known. I'll do whatever I can for you, but you must understand that it's Maria's choice and her choice alone that will count.'

Felipe agreed, 'I would not want it any other way.' He

119

turned his head in that moment to look sharply behind him, then added in a low whisper, 'Someone is coming this way. I will see you tomorrow. *Boa noite.*'

The next moment he had gone and a tall figure loomed before her.

'So, like myself, you are taking a walk before retiring, Diane,' Alonso murmured softly, looking down into her.

It occurred to her in those breathless moments that Felipe had known that it had been Alonso who had interrupted their tête-à-tête and had acted accordingly in making himself scarce in order to avoid any embarrassment. A newly risen moon was showing enough light for them to see each other clearly. And meeting those mocking eyes Diane saw the knowledge of her embarrassment in them. The blood rose hot in her cheeks. How hateful he was, with his cynicism! He had seen Felipe, of course—or if he had not then he had heard their voices and come to his own conclusion. The knowledge that she was not the kind of girl he took her to be only made her feel inexperienced and totally at a loss to know how to deal with him.

With a determined effort, she managed to appear uncaring and replied on a flippant note:

'As it's a pleasure which I'm now denied at home because it isn't safe, I naturally revel in the thought of being able to stroll unmolested and breathe in this lovely pine-scented air,' she told him lightly.

Her quick upward glance encountered an unreadable expression in his dark eyes. Disapproval, anger, dislike? Maybe it was none of those things, but it set her heart beating in a way that hurt. He would have a cause to be more angry with her now. From now on her friendship with Felipe would make her more unforgivable in his eyes than the girl who had influenced his sister to defy him.

He said slowly and vibrantly, 'While I share your desire for a walk I hardly think it is wise for you to leave a heated room and go right into the night air minus an extra wrap. At this high altitude, the mist is apt to be very chill to body warmth. I suggest you cut your walk short and return indoors.'

His fingers closed on her arm and that light firm touch of his hand sent a heat through her body. 'I'm quite warm enough,' she protested.

'All the same, we had better go indoors.' His tone brooked no refusal and Diane walked by his side aware of that hand burning her flesh with the knowledge that she was head over heels in love with a man who despised her.

When they entered the Quinta, she hoped the increased colour in her cheeks would go unnoticed, but she need not have worried, for Alonso barely glanced down at her as he wished her goodnight. As she went to her room Diane had qualms about the game she was playing with Felipe. Alonso would not take lightly to it, since he would be there most of the time to see what was going on. Her face was set, her eyes unhappy as she prepared for bed. It wasn't going to be easy, but Alonso might not be there. She knew nothing of his plans during their visit, which was only a weekend as far as she knew. So much the better if he was not there. However, that was something that her head told her. Her heart denied it and said something very different.

CHAPTER SEVEN

WITHIN the cool dark interior of the English church Diane gazed up at the gilded Baroque splendour that character-ised many of the churches on the island. The congregation was composed of the local people and a few visitors. Through the tall windows bars of shadow slanted across the black mantillas of the local women and the dark suits of the men. The domed ceiling was beautifully and richly em-bossed in gold, catching shafts of light which shed torch-like beams in the cloistered air. Felipe's golden hair seemed to be entangled in the sun's rays as he stood by his aunt Luisa, who wore fine black lace over her hair.

What doubts Diane might have had in offering to help the lovelorn Felipe were charmed away by him. There was no denying that he was a very likeable person. He had wit, charm, and the kind of blond good looks that contrasted sharply with Alonso's dark features. It was obvious that Felipe was very much in love with Maria, for he made little effort to hide the fact. His charming smile faded when she persisted in evading his adoring glances, but his face, though betraying his unhappiness, was never hard or cyni-cal. He was a nice young man who had fallen in love and was being repulsed.

Maria was aware of his devotion—Diane was sure of that. It was the reason for her being so resentful of him, why, every so often, her hostility flared and was as quickly extinguished. A Valmardi could not be openly rude with the Duque around. On their return to the Quinta Alonso was met by one of his stewards from the Valmardi estate with a message, leaving Felipe with the two girls, the two older ladies having gone for some recipes from the kitchen promised to the Senhora de Valmardi on her last visit.

Felipe said, all smiles, 'Perhaps you would like to see around the farm. There have been several interesting additions since you were here, Maria.'

But Maria pouted stubbornly. 'Take Diane. I feel like a lazy morning. Besides, all that sun is not good for my head.'

Felipe looked nonplussed and eyed her with a pained expression. 'You never used to bother about the sun. Or is it me that you do not want to bother about?'

He looked so hurt that Diane felt bound to intervene. 'I shall be delighted to go round the farm with you, Felipe,' she said, smiling up at him brightly. 'Maria did have a bad head last evening and she must be anxious for it not to return.'

Diane had not wanted to go alone around the farm with Felipe, although she enjoyed his company. It would have been much better for Maria to go with them and thus give her the opportunity of leaving her alone with Felipe. But Maria was being tiresome and she felt like shaking her. She was in no mood either for Alonso, who came indoors as she was leaving with Felipe.

Alonso raised a black eyebrow as he saw that Maria was not with them.

Felipe said solicitously, 'I trust the messenger did not bring bad news, Alonso?'

The wide shoulders were lifted with a careless nonchalance, but the dark eyes were keen. 'Nothing that cannot wait until my return,' he answered. 'Are you going out?'

Felipe inclined his blond head as his good humour slowly returned.

'I am taking Diane around the farm. Maria did not wish to risk the sun giving her a bad head,' he explained with a smile.

Alonso's dark eyes moved from one face to the other, and Diane wished she knew what he was thinking. His absence had left her feeling normal. Now her heart was leaping again and doing the usual strange things it invariably did in his presence. For the moment, however, Alonso appeared to have other matters on his mind, for he did not appear to notice her telltale blush as he gave them a brief nod of dismissal.

It was a relief to move away from his presence, and Felipe was a pleasant antidote for him. The next hour went on wings, for Felipe was entertaining, intelligent and good company. And their being thrown together had not been planned, it had just happened, so Diane gave herself up to the enjoyment of the present. The tour of the farm was a condensed one, because the estate was large and there was too much to see in a few hours. It was enough to take in at a glance the vineyards, banana plantations, the fields of maize, sweet potatoes and other vegetables set out in patchwork precision.

The baby lambs were a delight and were a surprise to Diane, as were the fields filled with cows. One did not see them very often on the island. Felipe explained that most Madeiran farmers had to keep their cattle indoors because the deep gorges and ravines made it unsafe for them to wander. There were magnificent black pigs in their sties and ducks, geese and hens picking up food in large open pens outdoors. And Diane returned from the tour with a bunch of wild flowers in her arms.

The sun was hot that afternoon and even the altitude did not detract from its power. The two older ladies preferred to spend the afternoon indoors and Felipe had gone off somewhere with Alonso, leaving the two girls to amuse themselves. Maria had not fully recovered her humour after lunch and was sleeping in a lounger on the lawn in the shade of giant trees.

Diane, bemused by the beauty of the gardens, was apt to wander round despite the heat. There were glades with small ponds, fountains and streams set among velvet lawns, sunken gardens, flower beds, pergolas smothered in clematis, and breathtaking drifts of magnolia blossom filling the air with a heady perfume, and the song of birds. She had sat on the edge of a stone fountain to watch frogs frolicking up and down among the waterlilies and was bending down to pick up a massive magnolia blossom from the lawn when a shadow fell between her and the sun.

With her small hands hidden beneath the velvet petals, Diane looked up startled to see Alonso gazing down at her. His dark eyes lingered on hair holding liquid fire from the sun in its depths, eyes that were deep pools of wonder between long silken lashes and a soft pink mouth showing a glimpse of milk-white teeth. The smooth peach-like bloom of her skin deepened into rose and her graceful poise was a thing of beauty.

'Why did I not bring a camera?' he said with a half smile. 'And why are you alone? Surely Maria should be with you explaining the different species which, no doubt, are strange to you in the garden? Is it because a black head has more respect for the sun than a certain red-gold one? Come, let us stroll in the shade.'

Diane walked by his side into the shade of the trees with her legs not feeling quite steady. One word from him and I do exactly what he says, she told herself despairingly. She looked down at the purity of the flower in her hands and remembered what he had said about her being a bad influence on Maria. Yet it did not stop her loving him. The silence between them was louder than words and she was terribly conscious of his nearness. It was making her tonguetied.

'Here we have the bird of paradise flowers,' he said at last, pausing by a flower bed of exotic flowers in flame, orange and blue. 'Portuguese gardeners usually plant them for luck, and the superstitious ones will only plant trees at certain phases of the moon.'

'Do you share their superstitions?' she asked, gazing up at him with clear eyes. 'I would say that the Portuguese are very superstitious. I was thinking of the eye looking down at us in church, or is that supposed to ward off evil?'

'A bit of both,' he replied, his eyes lingering on her glowing face. 'You are looking much better since you came to the island. You like it here?'

To her dismay he was leading her towards a pergola of clematis where a white marble seat rested under its shade. Diane waited until he had seated her before taking the far corner of the seat himself. Hitching up the creases of his immaculate trousers, he half turned her way and waited for her answer. The scented atmosphere, like the beauty of their surroundings, seemed unruffled and Diane hoped that the only jarring unease was sensed only by herself. In company Alonso was attentive, polite and appeared concerned that she should enjoy her visit as much as possible. But at times he wore a curiously guarded expression which, when they were alone, held her at arm's length. Not that they were alone very often—which set her wondering why he had sought her out.

She thought he looked exactly as he had looked on that first day she had seen him on the steps of the hotel in Funchal, sun-tanned and glowing, his dark crisp hair in a slight disarray in the breeze, his whole appearance endowed with something swift, eager and vital. His face now held no flicker of emotion beyond normal interest.

'I like it very much,' she admitted at length on an inward sigh. 'This beauty kind of grows on one, and the climate is delicious.' Her chuckle was low and sweet at the frown flitting on his face. 'I feel that delicious is the correct word to use, since when I drink my coffee or fruit juice in the mornings it seems to me that the golden morning is also sliding down my throat.'

He nodded, and continued to stare at her.

'Have I a smut on my nose?' she was driven into saying as the seconds sped by and her colour mounted beneath his intent regard.

'I find it hard to believe that you have no suitor back home,' he said cynically. 'That bright hair, those clear eyes, your pleasing musical laugh, your voice surely found an echo in at least one young man's heart?'

'I'm afraid I can't satisfy your curiosity by admitting that I've known lots of conquests of the opposite sex. I can only say that what conquests I had never meant anything to me because I wasn't in search of a husband. I was too fond of my work. I loved it.'

He placed an arm along the back of the seat, bringing the long brown fingers very near beneath the immaculate cuff, and Diane resisted a temptation to touch his hand. The last thing she wanted was for him to see that, in spite of her outward tranquillity, her cool voice, she was striving to hide her unease in his company. She watched a butterfly settle on the clematis covering the pergola in front of her and felt some of her self-possession winging away with it when it moved on.

'Did it ocur to you when you came to the island that you might find a husband here?' he murmured.

Diane turned slowly to look at him, at the dark face and glittering eyes, and a sense of chill mounted to anger. As her anger rose she knew that this kind of situation was noththing new, since he had a capacity to provoke all kinds of emotions in her.

'What are you suggesting?' she demanded on a slight quiver. 'You think I'm making a pass at Felipe, don't you?'

Unabashed, he said, 'It did occur to me.'

'Did it?' By now Diane was fairly sizzling with wrath. Her face paled and she bit on her lip hard to steady it. 'I'm not surprised, since you regard me as game for anything, even to stealing my best friend's intended. Come to think of it, you could be right. It all fits in. I turn Maria against Felipe by letter, then wangle an invitation to come here and meet him. I like what I see, so I go ahead with my diabolical plans. Too bad that the only diabolical plans are your own, to—to force your sister into marriage so that you can be free of any sense of obligation in order to marry yourself!

'This is most interesting,' he said tersely. 'Do go on. Tell me more. Whom do I plan to marry?'

Diane rose to her feet and looked down with remorse at the magnolia flower as it fluttered to the ground from her knee. She had forgotten all about picking it up. Now it lay discarded and broken, a symbol of her own fate at the hands of a man who had not the slightest inkling of what love meant.

'I'm not interested,' she bit out as hurt gave way to fresh anger. 'In any case, while it's no business of mine whom you marry, it's no business of yours whom I marry either.'

'It is my business if you marry Felipe. He is not a man of the world like myself and has not travelled from the island. He is bemused with you—you are so different from the Portuguese. I have seen him looking very different when he is with you. When you went on the tour of the farm and when you returned with your arms filled with flowers you had the look of the English girl, eager, untrammelled, free of the inhibitions of the Portuguese woman. So you caught at Felipe's heart. His eyes said that he loved you and wanted you.' Alonso had been talking quickly and his voice took on a strange slightly thick undertone. 'I find it incomprehensible that you should deliberately hurt Maria and all of us with such actions.'

Diane stiffened as she gazed down unseeingly at the flower on the ground. Hurt all of them, he had said, including himself. Surely not? Nothing Diane McNair did could hurt him. Yet he just admitted that it was so. How could she tell him now that Felipe and she had planned to make Maria jealous? Even if she did and Felipe confirmed it he would find the whole idea distasteful and most unwomanly on her part. Furthermore, he would know that the idea had been her own since Felipe would not risk the reputation of a woman to further his own ends among his own people. Consequently Alonso would still question her motives. Better to allow him to think the worst of her—he always had done. This was the end of her visit to the island. She felt bruised and helpless and entirely alone. Even Maria seemed to have drawn away from her in a world of her own. And Alonso—he would never be friends with her; he had never even liked her. With such thoughts plunging her into the utter depths of misery, Diane threw constraint to the winds.

'I can see that I was wrong to come to the island. Your ways and mine are so different. I might have had a chance of

128

coming to a kind of compromise had you not disliked me from the start. I shall leave when we return to the Quinta de Valmardi.' Her hands were clenched by her sides and she drew a deep breath to steady her words. 'In the meantime you will oblige me by saying nothing as yet to Maria. Now, if you'll excuse me ...'

She stumbled away, narrowly missing treading on the magnolia flower at her feet, and made her way back to the Quinta. Maria was still asleep on the lawn and Diane reached her room in a lather of sweat. Leaning back against the closed doors, she closed her eyes. This time tomorrow she would be back at the Quinta de Valmardi and packing her things as quickly as possible. Until then she had to make the best of it. Felipe was giving a party for her that evening. It was an ordeal that she was not looking forward to, but it was surprising what one could do when one gave one's mind to it.

First she would take a bath and spend time on preparing herself for the party. No one would say that she had not gone down smiling. She would be radiant. The spell in perfumed water revived her wilted spirits, and applying two pieces of gauze soaked in witch hazel to her eyes, she slipped in between the cool sheets and tried to relax. A warm breeze drifted in softly through the open window, bringing with it a sweet scent of oleanders. The palm tree whispered and she slept.

It was dark when she awakened and a swift glance at the illuminated travelling clock on her bedside table told her that she had about half an hour to get ready for the party. So much for the time she was going to take in dressing! she thought with dismay, taking off the eye pads and dropping them into the waste paper basket. Her skin was perfumed from the bath and the quick application of a fragrant lotion over her body ensured a cool skin for the evening. Cobweb tights and cool silk underwear followed. Swiftly she polished her nails until they shone free of nail varnish and then massaged cream lightly into her face as a base for light make-up.

The dress, brought with her for the occasion, was in soft lavender chiffon with a figure-hugging bodice and full skirt. Diane had adored it on sight and had planned on wearing it on special occasions. Well, this occasion was special, the last party for her on the island. But there was no joy in seeing her own enchanting reflection in the dressing table mirror, no joy in the delicate soft folds billowing out from her youthfully slim waist and accentuating her feminine charms. Hastily she fastened a velvet choker around her slim throat, straightened the small cameo in front and added matching cameo studs to her ears. A scarf around her shoulders gave her full rein to brush the red-gold hair into the sheen of freshly minted copper before allowing it to fall into its naturally curly state. Then the final make-up, a whisper of eye-shadow above the touched-up long lashes, a delicately toned lipstick blending with the colour of her dress, and a light application of face powder. Silk court shoes and a black velvet bag to match the choker at her throat, and she was ready.

A last look in the mirror assured her that she was looking her best and, as guest of honour, she looked demure enough to satisfy Portuguese standards. But in her heart Diane knew that it was Alonso's approval which mattered above all else. However much he disapproved of her she would never get over her love for him.

Ready at last with a few minutes to spare before Maria called, Diane went to her window to gaze out at the view of hills and pines. The heat that had shimmered above the jagged edges of rocks in the dry brilliance of light before dark was cooled now in the silvery gleam of moonlight that bathed everywhere in a peaceful silver glow. Lucky Maria, she thought wistfully, to have been brought up where angry sounds were nothing more than the roar of mountain torrents, where violence only came with the winter storms and where the dignity of hills instilled in one an upright way of walking with a proud angle of the head.

When Maria came, her smooth velvet cheeks aglow, her soft youthful curves covered in a demure dress of primrose

130

silk, she exclaimed in admiration, 'How lovely you look, Diane! I love your dress.'

'Thank you, Maria—but you look far more beautiful than I do. How is the head? Quite well again, I hope?'

Diane looked at the exquisite face with concern. It seemed to her that Maria had lost that sweet assurance she had carried so demurely at their first meeting. She had changed and it had become more marked since they had arrived at the Quinta Moltano. Was it Felipe? Was she regretting repulsing his advances and was too proud to admit it? She was about to ask her point blank about him when Maria impulsively took her hands.

'My headache has gone,' she said. 'I am touched that you should be so concerned. You are happy we came on this visit?'

She was now the one who looked concerned. Diane squeezed her hands.

'Of course,' she replied. 'And you?'

'I am if you are.' Excitement began to sparkle in Maria's dark eyes. 'We are going to have a wonderful time this evening. Felipe has engaged a troupe of dancers to entertain us. Come on, we must not be late!'

They went down the stairs to find the hall a bower of flowers with the staff hurrying about their various duties unobtrusively yet with an air of excitement. The first person Diane saw as she entered the main *sala* was Alonso. He was talking to his mother, accompanied by Senhora Luisa and Felipe. Instantly Alonso's dark eyes captured her own across the space and there was a diversity of expression in them as they alighted on her face.

His tanned features, hawklike in the mellow light, held a lynx-like regard, acting as keen as the incision of a scalpel baring her heart. Was it interest, consideration or appraisal? She gave herself a little shake.

What a idiot she was to let her imagination run on so, when the Duque de Valmardi had nothing but contempt for Diane McNair who had interfered with his plans for his sister so dramatically! It was conceited of her to entertain the idea that he could be interested in anyone as ordinary as herself, even had he liked her. Her hair was a nice colour, but it was unfashionably curly and, in her own opinion, she looked quite insipid against Maria's magnolia beauty, her dark hair and flashing eyes.

Felipe came forward to greet them eagerly, his blond good looks proving an added attraction in evening dress. Diane was sure that this was not lost on Maria, although she assumed an air of polite indifference. The guests began to arrive, most of them young people around Diane's age and invited especially for her. She was seated on Felipe's right side at the dinner table with his younger brother Joao seated next to her.

Joao was as dark as Felipe was fair, with wide shoulders and the kind of short blunt figure which runs to fat in middle age. He helped to look after the family estates in Portugal, but was expecting to marry soon.

'Mother would be delighted to make your acquaintance, Miss McNair,' he said, looking at her in open admiration. 'She was English before her marriage.'

Diane murmured some kind of reply as the meal got under way with its many varied courses. As the waiters hovered two young men appeared in Portuguese costumes to sing *fados* eloquently and romantically, filling the air with the old Portuguese magic that still persisted on the island.

In a *sala* next to the dining room, coffee and liqueurs were served to the guests, who occupied the small tables and chairs set around the walls to give them a clear view of the centre of the floor. On to this cleared space came the *bailinho* dancers engaged by Felipe for the evening. Their traditional dances were exciting and colourful, with red skirts swirling, arms waving and white boots stamping out a dynamic rhythm. At the end of their performance they drew the guests from their chairs to join in the colourful, confetti-strewn procession round the *sala*. From there they all meandered out to the patio overlooking the gardens and sank breathless and laughing into white wicker furniture

132

placed to give them a view of the grounds. With much merriment they carried away a guy festooned in fireworks on to the lawns and, at a given signal from Felipe, fireworks were set off in a breathtaking display of colour.

The party was now riotously gay, with poinsettias, camellias and carnival streamers being thrown to the guests by the dancers. Diane enjoyed it immensely, although she could never quite ignore the fact of Alonso being present. He had been seated some distance away from her at the table and he had not once looked her way. Now he was seated at the far end of the patio with Senhora Luisa and his mother, and although she tried hard to ignore him, some-. how his vibrant personality seemed to touch her heart. It was obvious from the few glances she had sent his way during the evening that he was rather detached from the merry young people nearby. But he had joined in the lively procession around the *sala*, afterwards accepting a flower from one of the dancers to put in his buttonhole.

While Felipe was engaged in looking after his guests his brother Joao devoted himself to Diane. She was glad of the tenacity with which he clung to her, since it kept Alonso at bay, although she doubted if he knew she was there for all the notice he had taken of her. Maria mixed with the other guests, some of whom she had known for years, and her glances towards Diane were teasing at the sight of Joao paying her so much attention. During an interval in the evening entertainment, Maria came over to speak to her as she sat waiting for Joao to return with refreshments.

'I see that Joao is looking after you,' she said, sitting down in the chair he had just vacated. 'Felipe gives nice parties. Did you enjoy the dancers?'

'Very much. I've noticed how popular Felipe is with the *senhoritas*.' Diane smiled gently into Maria's dark eyes, thinking how pretty she looked. 'The *senhorita* he will eventually marry will be very lucky. I could fall in love with him myself quite easily.'

A pale rose colour crept beneath Maria's magnolia skin and she rose to her feet with a youthful dignity.

'I can see Joao coming with your refreshment,' she said hastily. 'Enjoy yourself. I will see you later.'

Joao ate his share of the food he had brought, but remarked on Diane's poor appetite as she nibbled at the delicacies.

'But I ate so much for dinner,' she protested. 'I'm just not hungry.'

'The food will bolster your morale,' Joao said darkly. 'Do not forget that you are the guest of honour.'

'What do you mean, Joao?' Diane eyed him with concern. 'Why are you looking so mysterious? If it's something about me surely I have a right to know? Come on, Joao, tell me,' she pleaded.

But Joao only smiled, finished the last tasty morsel on his plate, and picking up his glass of wine, gave her a look of undisguised admiration.

'I must not spoil the fun,' he said, and lifted his glass. 'Here is to the most beautiful *senhorita* I have had the pleasure of dining with for a long time. It is indeed my misfortune that you are leaving the Quinta so soon.'

The waiters came to take away the used dishes. Diane refused more wine and was suddenly aware of Felipe in conversation with Alonso at the far side of the *sala*. Aunt Luisa and Senhora de Valmardi were there too, forming a little group along with Maria. Presently a member of the staff entered and gave Felipe a small package. As he withdrew, Felipe held up his hand for the guests to be silent, then he began to speak.

'As you are all aware, it has been our great pleasure this evening to have the honour of entertaining Senhorita Maria de Valmardi's friend from England, Miss Diane McNair. To commemorate the occasion I wish to present her with a small token of our regard. Diane, will you please come forward?'

Dazedly Diane rose to her feet and crossed the *sala* to a burst of applause. She was not aware that her face was the colour of a rose beneath the aura of red-gold hair or that her smile was sweetly tremulous as she halted to gaze up at

134

Felipe. Her whisper was urgent and meant for Felipe's ears alone. 'This is not necessary, Felipe,' she said. 'I ought to be very annoyed with you.'

He laughed. 'For you, Diane, with our warmest love. Although we have a surfeit of flowers on the island I am sure, like my friends, that the addition of a lovely English rose in our midst is more than welcome.' he said soberly, and gave her the small parcel.

Diane thanked him and tiptoed to kiss his cheek to great applause and a few teasing remarks. Then Felipe was moving away and someone else was taking his place. She looked up, startled, into the dark face of Alonso, and her breath locked in her throat. To her eyes, somewhere below his jaw, the clean-cut structure of his face, the long slightly flaring nose and the well cut mouth took on a cool arrogance in the muted lighting. His eyes looked incredibly dark and much too attractive, she thought somewhat incoherently as he held up a hand for silence.

'I can only second what my friend Felipe has said,' he began as the brilliant white smile came into play. 'However, we Valmardis wish also to show our appreciation of Miss Diane's visit to our shores.' Here his eyes gleamed wickedly. 'Furthermore, on recalling Felipe's reward, I now present this small gift with the utmost pleasure.'

Someone made a polite boo as he presented the gift and he laughed. Diane clutched the two gifts convulsively as a silence that seemed charged with electricity settled all around her. The guests were waiting patiently for her to thank him ... with a kiss. She gathered her scattered wits, saw that there was no way out of it and lifted her face hurriedly to kiss his cheek.

The kiss landed somewhere in the region of the side of his jaw. Diane savoured his own particular fragrance of good grooming, after-shave lotion combined with the subtle fragrance of a good cigar, before turning blindly away. A storm of clapping broke out and Maria was kissing her.

Later, in her room, Diane knew a darkness of spirit dragging her down into an abyss as she laid the presents un-

135

opened on the dressing table and sank down into the nearest chair. She could still feel the barely perceptible touch of Alonso's fingers as he had given her the gift. His tones had been of the kind that, knowing the antagonism that existed between them, deliberately humoured her. And if she had been unprepared for his gift, she had been unprepared also for his nearness. It had aroused a hunger in her that she had found it hard to control. There had been a sudden urge to throw herself into his arms, to cling to him, to feel the utter bliss of his mouth upon her own. The longing and the anguish had been all the more unbearable because the present was meant by him to be a parting gift.

Diane could not blame him for wanting her to go. Indeed, she could find it in her poor bruised heart to admire him for it. His was a strength of character that went beyond the bounds of his magnetic personality and physical perfection. He possessed the kind of qualities a woman looked for in a man and found, if she was lucky. He was not perfect—what man was? But his faults were not vices. To one who adored him they were lovable faults because they were part of the beloved. Alonso was the partner she had always dreamed about, a man who was on the same wavelength as herself directly he entered the same room, a man who brought her vividly to life, a man who would remain forever in her heart although worlds might divide them. And he did not even like her. She leaned her head back against the chair and tears oozed from between her lashes. Some time between now and the next afternoon she had to tell Maria that she was leaving the island. There were many problems to face even after she had gone back home—the problem of writing to Maria and hearing all the news, including Alonso's marriage. She had hoped sincerely that brother and sister did not remain hopelessly stubborn, stubborn enough to keep both of them from marrying.

A tap on her door made her reach hastily for her handkerchief to dab her eyes and give her nose a small blow to clear the air, as it were. It was Maria.

'I had to come in to see you,' she said. 'Something ter-

136

rible has happened. Bella Vangroot has been involved in a fire at her *quinta*. A messenger has just brought Alonso the news. My brother wants us to be ready to start for home early in the morning.'

'That's dreadful! Is she hurt at all?'

'I do not think so, but I believe the *quinta* has been extensively damaged.' Maria sat down rather dejectedly on the bed. 'I suppose this will bring matters to a head between them'.

Diane swallowed on a dry throat. 'You mean—they'll get married?' she asked huskily.

Maria shrugged. 'Your guess is as good as mine. The trouble is nobody seems to know what Alonso's intentions are, not even Mother.'

She stared down dejectedly at the carpet and Diane, perforce, did the same. Then Maria brightened as though prompted by a thought.

'What about your presents? Have you unwrapped them yet? If so, may I see them?'

Diane started guiltily. 'I haven't looked at them yet, so we can undo them together. It's awfully kind of you all, but I feel it's I who should give presents since you've all been so kind to me.'

She moved to the dressing table and gave one of the gifts to Maria.

'You can unwrap Felipe's present,' she said with forced gaiety. 'You've probably seen the other.'

Diane sat down again and began to unwrap the small packet, to reveal a long jewel case. As she pressed the catch to open it Maria said rather offhandedly, 'I have not seen either of them. Alonso had your present sent from the jewellers in Funchal. What is it?' She leaned forward eagerly to see Diane staring at what lay inside the case.

'It's a wristwatch. It's beautiful, and far too valuable for me to wear. I shall be afraid of losing it,' Diane gasped.

Maria gazed at the exquisite wristwatch in diamonds and platinum as if it was a most ordinary present. 'Of course you will not be anything of the kind,' she said scornfully.

'Alonso will have insured it for you. It is like mine—see, he bought this for my birthday last year. It keeps wonderful time. I think it is the ideal present for you, because we are like sisters and it is only right that you should have the same things as I.' She held up a slim wrist to show the wrist-watch in queston.

Then she leaned forward to hug Diane before unwrapping the other gift. The present from Felipe was a necklace of silver and precious stones. The setting was exquisite, the silverwork beautiful in an attractive dark shading effect which gave a mellowed look to the embossed flowers.

'Well,' Maria commented when she lifted her eyes from the case, 'I would agree that he deserved the kiss!'

'You didn't mind me kissing him, did you, Maria? We always do that back home when we receive a present from either sex,' Diane assured her earnestly. 'We think nothing of it.'

'Why should I mind?' Maria was suddenly flippant. She passed the present to Diane and rose to her feet. 'I had better go to bed, if we are to start early in the morning.'

She drifted to the door, and Diane felt an urge to know the truth about her friend's feelings for Felipe.

'Maria, wait!' she cried, then stopped, for the face Maria turned her way was a closed one. The expression in the dark eyes reminded her in that moment of Alonso's way of looking through her. 'It doesn't matter,' she added.

Maria shrugged slim shoulders and went quietly from the room. It was not until she had gone that Diane realised that she had not mentioned her plan to leave on their return to the Quinta de Valmardi.

CHAPTER EIGHT

THEY left early the following morning, and the leavetaking was overcast by the news of Bella Vangroot. Alonso looked grim, his mother looked worried, and Maria was stony-faced. Felipe and Senhora Luisa were much concerned to hear of the bad news and asked Alonso to keep them informed.

At the last moment Diane slipped a note into Felipe's hand telling him that she would give him news of Maria when she could. She thought wryly that it would come from the letters she received when Maria wrote to her after she had left the island. She had not the heart to tell Felipe of her intention to do so.

Alonso drove at speed as if he could not wait to go to Bella's aid. Maria was non-committal during the journey and the Senhora only passed mundane remarks from time to time as she respected her son's concern for his friend.

Had Diane not been feeling so miserable she would have winced at the way Alonso cut precipitous bends. Instead she kept her eyes averted from the back of that well-shaped head and told herself that he had forgotten already that Diane McNair had ever existed. They were about half way on their journey when Alonso said, 'We had better make a detour and call on Bella to see if there is anything that we can do.'

No one answered, so he took their silence for consent and veered the big car round to take another road. When they arrived the drive was quiet and they met no one. Then they saw the *quinta*, or rather what was left of it. Part of the roof had gone and the front was a blackened shell.

Alonso switched off the car engine, and for several moments they all sat silent and staring aghast at the *quinta*. The Senhora was the first to speak.

'I will come in with you, Alonso,' she said gently. 'If Bella is still here she will need a friend. The girls can stay in the car.'

Alonso left his seat and strode around the car to help his mother out.

When they had entered the *quinta*, Maria said fiercely, 'I would not put it past Bella to have started the fire herself. She will do anything to get Alonso to propose.'

Diane turned to her in surprise. 'Surely not, Maria? I'm sure Bella would never do a thing like that. The amount of damage is considerable and it will take an enormous amount of money to put it right. I can't see Bella taking a chance like that, unless ...'

She stopped, unable to voice her thoughts further. But Maria took her up swiftly.

'Exactly,' she cried. 'Unless she is sure of Alonso. Oh no! What did I tell you? Do you see what I see?'

Maria had paled and was staring ahead through the windscreen of the car. Diane followed her gaze to see Alonso coming from the *quinta* carrying Bella in his arms. Senhora de Valmardi came after him and hastened to open the car door. The next moment Alonso was placing Bella in the front seat and was covering her with a rug. Then he opened the other door and helped his mother into the back seat with Maria and Diane.

'Bella collapsed when she saw us,' the Senhora whispered hurriedly by way of explanation. 'Everything is in a dreadful mess and the poor girl could not possibly stay here with things as they are, so we are taking her back to the *quinta*.'

Maria's glance at Diane was a 'What did I tell you?' one and they did not answer. Bella lay back in her seat with an air of exhaustion as Alonso put on speed. His concerned glances her way were refined torture to Diane, who was still debating whether it was possible that Bella had really started the fire in order to bring matters to a head between her and Alonso. And had he in turn given Bella reason to believe that he meant to marry her? If this was so then the sooner she left the island the better for her own peace of mind.

On their arrival Alonso carried Bella into the quinta to the flurried goings and comings of the already alerted staff. As if in a vacuum, Diane noticed how becoming the uniform of the staff was, with the collar and cuffs enhanced by a covering of white embroidery. The moderately high collar gave a sense of dignity to the wearer. Their cases were carried in and the Senhora hurriedly left the car to give instructions to the staff concerning the unexpected guest.

As they left the car Maria laid a hand urgently upon Diane's arm, to guide her away from the quinta entrance.

'Come,' she whispered urgently. 'We need to talk and map out our campaign against this latest move of Bella's. Let us sit beneath the silver tree in the garden where we can be alone. I used to make wishes there when I was a child. I always felt it had a kind of magic.'

Maria's eagerness, her impetuosity was so like that of a child that Diane wanted to hug her and be stern with her at the same time. The shock of seeing Alonso actually carrying Bella into the quinta must have made the poor child light in the head, she thought commiseratingly.

'All right,' she told her firmly. 'So long as you go no further than wishing. There's nothing more you can do. If Alonso has set his mind on marrying Bella, you'll just have to accept it.'

But Maria did not seem to hear. She dragged Diane down on the seat beneath the lovely silver tree and said forcefully, 'I shall make a bargain with Alonso. If he will give me his word that he will not marry Bella, I will accede to his wishes and marry Felipe. Do you not think that is a good idea, Diane?'

Diane looked at the trusting dark eyes and smiled gently as she shook her head.

'That would hardly be fair, would it?' she replied, 'since it would be no hardship for you to marry Felipe. You're very fond of him—and don't try to deny it. And maybe for Alonso to give you such a promise could mean heartbreak for him if he loves Bella. So you see, you can't do this to your brother, Maria. You're too kindhearted to wish to hurt him in any way.'

'And I thought you were my friend. You are not my friend or you would say differently,' Maria cried accusingly.

'It's because I'm saying this that I am your friend. I wouldn't continue to be so had I advised you differently, Maria. You must see that.'

'Then what are we to do?'

Maria looked at her piteously, and Diane shook her head. She said slowly.

'I'm sorry, Maria, but I hate to tell you this at such a time. I'm leaving the quinta today. My cases are already packed and I think it's time I should go. I've enjoyed my visit to you immensely, and it's been lovely meeting you at last after all these years.'

Maria's face paled. 'But why now, Diane? You have not been here long enough to see everything there is to see on the island, and I have not shown you off to all my friends yet.'

Suddenly the tears were falling down her cheeks and she took Diane's hands in her trembling ones. She was beyond words.

Diane was touched more than she cared to admit. Taking the small hands closely in her warm grasp, she said, 'Maria darling, don't cry like this. I have to leave some time, and why not now? After all, you have another guest in the quinta now. I shall only be in the way.'

Maria withdrew a hand to find a handkerchief to dry her tears, and sniffed audibly.

'You cannot desert me now in my hour of need,' she said thickly. 'I shall die if you go away now and leave me alone with that woman.'

'But you won't be alone with her. You have your mother and Alonso,' Diane reminded her gently. 'Besides, you're surmising that the worst is going to happen. It might never do so.'

'You are only saying that to comfort me. You do not really believe it. Oh, please do not go yet, dear Diane. Please stay,' Maria pleaded.

Diane looked into the tear-wet eyes and was lost. With

clear-eyed honesty and swift intuitive sympathy she knew that by giving in to Maria and staying on even for a short time would mean much pain for herself. Her hands now free of Maria's entreating clasp felt as chilled and bloodless as her heart. To stay on at the Quinta, to see Alonso's tender ministrations to the woman he loved, would be torture beyond bearing. Yet that was what she was going to do, because Maria needed her. Already she was shrinking from the ordeal ahead, but her resolution did not waver.

'All right,' she said. 'I'll stay if it means so much to you, dear Maria. But you must promise me one thing, and that is not to upset yourself if what you are dreading really does happen.'

Maria promised eagerly enough and her gratitude was touching. 'We will go out often, you and I,' she promised, already looking brighter. 'We will leave Alonso so much with his Bella that he will become heartily sick of her. Come, let us go indoors and make our plans.'

The Quinta de Valmardi took on a new atmosphere with Bella Vangroot there. It seemed to Diane that the staff were more withdrawn, as if they sensed the atmosphere also as being not so free and easy. They were too dedicated to their job to be slack or careless in any way, but there was a kind of tightening up which Diane sensed to be almost tangible. A doctor had been sent for to examine Bella soon after she had arrived and he had assured Alonso that the *senhorita* was merely suffering from shock and that it was wise to keep her from the sight of her damaged *quinta* until such time as she had completely recovered. Diane thought Alonso looked a little tensed up, which was unusual for him, and her heart contracted in putting it down to his concern over Bella. Bella did not appear at dinner that evening of her arrival but stayed in her room, and the meal passed off without incident. After dinner, while Maria and her mother pored over the recipes from Felipe's Aunt Luisa, Diane took a short stroll in the garden. Alonso had left the *sala* immediately after dinner and

143

Diane tried not to think of him sitting with Bella. It would be a relief if he did announce their engagement, she thought unhappily. At least there would then be no more conjecturing at what was going to happen.

The thought of Alonso married to Bella was agony, the uncertainty an anguish that was tearing her apart. With her heart turning over sickeningly in her breast she found herself by the silver tree and sank down on to the seat. Maria said that wishes made under the tree came true. Yet how could she wish for a love that now seemed to be sunk into doubt and despair?

'So I find you beneath Maria's favourite tree. Are you making a wish or merely taking in the night air?'

Alonso's deep drawl had the effect of an electric shock to Diane's whole system. Her nerves tingled and her hands dovetailed painfully in her lap as she looked up at him looming over her. He was looking down at her with his lean arrogant features relaxing into the semblance of a smile. There was nothing tense about him now; indeed he looked almost happy. But of course, the presence of his lady love in the Quinta could account for that. Diane told herself that she did not care, for this very short space of time stolen from the lap of the gods was hers to share with Alonso whom she loved more than anyone else in the world.

She said, not very steadily, 'The pleasure of being able to stroll in the night air and feel safe from any possible attacker is still a luxury in which I love to indulge. I hope Senhorita Vangroot is feeling much improved, although little can be done for her *quinta*.'

'Bella is as well as can be expected in the circumstances,' he replied, pushing his hands into his pockets and regarding her downbent head thoughtfully. 'I am going to look at the damage and assess the cost of restoring the place. To my mind what little I saw of it entirely rules out such a procedure. Far better to knock the place down and rebuild it.'

Diane shot him a startled look and dropped her gaze again swiftly.

'But won't that cost a great deal of money, besides putting the Senhorita temporarily out of a home?' she exclaimed.

He shrugged. 'I have forbidden her to return to it as it is. The place is not safe. I have sent for a man well versed on such matters from Funchal to go over it. There will be a great deal of work involved in salvaging everything from the ruins, and the cause of the fire is yet to be established.'

'You mean no one knows yet what caused it?'

'No one. Bella has an idea that it could have started in the kitchens. One of the staff could have been careless about the fire.' He paused, then added, 'I would appreciate it if you would be friends with her during this unfortunate time. She is in the unenviable situation of being obliged to accept whatever hospitality is offered to her. I take it that you have changed your mind about leaving?'

'For the present,' she answered evenly. 'Maria insists upon me seeing more of the island before I leave and I have no wish to upset her. I trust my decision to stay meets with your approval, since you have asked a favour of me.'

Although Diane had not lifted her eyes she knew that he was considering her downbent head in silence.

'Why not?' his tone was dry, and there was no warmth in it as he went on. 'You are quite different from what I expected from your influence over Maria. Since I have had time to study you I have come to the conclusion that Maria's own wilfulness is responsible for her attitude towards Felipe. You are really a romantic at heart as she is, and not at all the kind of person who has been initiated into your English Women's Lib. Am I right?'

Diane lifted her eyes a trifle and avoided looking into his dark probing gaze. 'And if you are, does it make any difference? The majority of English girls lead decent ordinary lives and, strangely enough, remain detached from all the permissiveness going on around them. They are

145

even as demure and as feminine as your Portuguese *senhoritas*. You would be surprised.'

Her voice was laden with sarcasm, an armour used against his slightly patronising air which hardened her for a moment.

'I am sure I would,' he agreed. 'I admit to having misjudged you. I hope you will forgive me.' He made a slight bow which Diane found rather supercilious in its arrogance.

How dared he be so stuffy with her? Anger rose inside her and she stared up at him to see his dark eyebrows raised slightly. For once his coolly arrogant regard, which usually embarrassed her, now had the effect of putting her on her mettle.

'You mean that there's to be a kind of compromise between us? I would welcome that, especially since you've been against me from the day I arrived.'

His eyebrows lifted a little further and he smiled. 'You are mistaken, for if that were so, then there will certainly be no compromise between us. Compromise is not possible in love or in war. It is always a fight to the end.'

He was gazing down at her with his white arrogant smile. His height, his wide shoulders and dark features momentarily blotted out the background against which he stood. Diane went cold. She had a feeling that he knew how she felt about him and was taunting her as he must have taunted other women who had been dazzled by his charms. The silence between them seemed to stretch into eternity.

Then he said, 'Did you like your present?'

'Yes, thank you, but it was not necessary to give me a present, even though you intended it for a going away gift. I suppose you thought nothing was too much to pay to be rid of me.'

He straightened, his back rigid with anger, his face and voice tight.

'You must be under some misapprehension,' he said quietly. 'I presume that you have not questioned Felipe's gift? Then why question mine?'

Diane sat there feeling the cool mountain air on her

warm cheeks, then she said in a tight but very controlled little voice, 'I would like to ask you a question.'

'What is it?' and his voice was more controlled and colder than her own.

'If I had not told you when I did that I was going home, would you still have given me an expensive gift?'

He frowned down at her for long moments, then said firmly, 'Of course. And I do not understand this word "expensive". We are not beggars, nor peasants, we are people of means. As such we are not in the habit of giving paltry presents. We are also of good breeding and we have a code of behaviour which we live up to—always.'

'You're telling me! Diane murmured under her breath. Now where do we go from here? she asked herself despairingly.

Aloud, she said, 'I'm sorry, it seems I owe you an apology. Only please not another present when I leave. I couldn't accept it.'

Stiffly he replied, 'We will leave that until the time comes for you to go. And now I think it will be wise for you to go indoors before you become too chilled with the falling temperature. It can be quite something here in the hills even in summer.'

Diane rose to her feet and he walked with her in silence to the Quinta, stepping politely to one side to allow her to enter before him. She did not take her leave of him in any words but made straight for the staircase and the haven of her own room. The Senhora and Maria would think it odd that she had not looked in the *sala* to wish them goodnight, but she did not care. Another brush with the Duque de Valmardi like this one would absolutely be the last straw. In fact Diane was not quite sure whether this last one already was.

But life took on a different aspect the next morning when she awoke. The memory of her conversation the previous evening could not lightly be forgotten, and she only had one defence, to behave as though it had never happened. Fortunately Alonso had left early to go to the Vangroot *quinta* which made it easier for her to put her plan into action.

Senhora de Valmardi was on her own when Diane went down to breakfast. She was looking through her mail and greeted her with a warm smile.

'Maria was fast asleep when I looked in some moments ago,' she said. 'I'm worried about her. She seems to be so highly strung these days. What with Alonso going about like a cat on hot bricks too, I really don't feel myself any more.' She sighed and lifted the silver coffee pot to pour out two cups of steaming fragrant coffee. 'Now we have Bella to contend with. Alonso has gone this morning to see the extent of the damage. One thing is certain—Bella won't be going back until something is done.'

Diane accepted her cup of coffee with a smile. 'Not to mention another extra guest—myself. It all puts extra work on the staff. If there's anything I can do to help ...'

Her voice trailed off, leaving an opening for the Senhora to pave the way for her own visit to be curtailed on the excuse that the older woman had enough to contend with without her daughter's friend staying on indefinitely. But the Senhora's reaction to this was to exclaim sincerely,

'I'm more than grateful for your presence here, Diane. It's a great comfort to me. As for causing the staff extra work, I can assure you that we've always maintained above our quota to cope with parties and any other entertainment. We entertained a great deal when my husband was alive, and our guests included some very distinguished people. So you see that your presence here doesn't constitute any hardship in that direction.'

Diane topped her egg, gazed down at the golden yolk, and took up her spoon.

'I suppose you'll entertain again when Alonso marries,' she said, and managed a smile.

Characteristically, the Senhora shrugged her shoulders. 'I now don't think that the day will not be far off when he announces his engagement. Somehow I think this fire at the Vangroot residence has precipitated things. I have

148

noticed that Alonso, who is always so urbane, so serene, has been on edge of late, and I can't put it down to anything else. I've never known him to be like this before.'

Diane swallowed a spoonful of egg and lifted a crisp brown roll covered in golden butter. Her appetite was slowly diminishing. Her throat felt blocked with emotion, and she eyed the roll with some speculation.

'Alonso is probably worried about Maria,' she said. 'He's disappointed because she won't marry Felipe. He—he also wants to see her settled before he commits himself to anything.'

The Senhora raised finely pencilled brows. 'Alonso told you that? You should feel honoured. He doesn't usually take anyone into his confidence,' she remarked wryly. 'I don't suppose he has said anything about his own plans?'

Diane's face went a becoming pink. She said quickly, 'I'm not in Alonso's confidence—rather the reverse. He only told me about his wish that Maria should marry Felipe. It was Maria who told me that her brother was waiting to see her settled down before he married.'

The Senhora nodded. 'I can understand that,' she conceded. 'What I can't understand is Alonso's friendship with Bella. While we've always been friends with the Vangroots, we were never close. Indeed, until a year ago I doubt if Alonso was aware of Bella's existence half the time.'

'Does the Senhorita live alone at her *quinta*?' Diane asked, and bit valiantly into her buttered roll.

'Since her father died a year ago. Bella's mother died some years ago. Her father never married again, but he entertained lavishly and when he died the estate had been very neglected. Alonso put in a good manager and the estate was just picking up when the fire came. Now I doubt if Bella has the means to rebuild the *quinta*.'

Diane said, 'Alonso has asked me to be friends with Bella. I see she hasn't come down to breakfast. Is she any better?'

'She asked for breakfast at ten this morning. I shall send a tray to her room and call later to ask about her.'

'May I take her tray when breakfast is over? She's no doubt feeling miserable at the change in her fortunes. I hope she manages to salvage all the little sentimental things that mean so much to a person who has lost her family.'

The Senhora leaned across the table to pat Diane on the hand.

'What a sweet person you are,' she said warmly. 'I'm sure Bella will appreciate it. She's not an easy person to know, but Alonso seems to bring out the best in her.'

The Senhora did not say whether she liked Bella, or not, but Diane had the feeling that she was not very keen on her. Bella's personal maid had already taken up the breakfast tray when Diane asked for it, and it was some time later when she made her way to her room.

Bella was sitting up in bed when Diane entered. The breakfast tray had been cleaned away and her maid, a grim-looking woman of around forty, let her in and left the room. Bella's face was sallow but delicately made up, her black hair was immaculately combed back with the gleam of a comb above her head at the back. Her black eyes were enigmatic but her long hands on the coverlet were restless as she gazed at her visitor.

Diane could not admit what she felt towards her in that first moment. She found it impossible to forget what Maria had said about her being responsible for the fire at her *quinta*, or that her own jealousy contributed to the fact that she was inclined to agree. She wished that all the mystery was cleared up, and a great weariness assailed her.

'How are you?' she asked brightly. 'I'm so sorry. It must have been a great ordeal for you.'

Bella shrugged. 'It might have been had not Alonso been here to help me,' she said with no particular expression in her voice. 'He is the most fantastic man I have ever known. Already he has plans for the *quinta* if it is beyond restoring.'

'Really?' Diane exclaimed, every nerve tingling as jealousy consumed her whole being. She braced herself for what was coming, not liking the malevolent gleam in the dark eyes.

Bella smoothed the top sheet on the bed and lowered her eyes as she went on. 'Yes. You see, my estate borders that of Alonso's and he has plans for uniting it with his since he means to expand. I am all in favour of it, since what I have will be his in any case later.'

Diane shuddered inwardly at the victorious lilt in her voice. If Alonso had not proposed to her already he would soon do so, for Bella was here in his *quinta* and, beyond all doubting, she would continue to remain until she had achieved her objective. Poor Maria, she thought, and poor Alonso, for she could not in all truth see him happy with such a schemer. But it was none of her business, and she could not for the life of her see what Alonso was concerned about in asking her to be friends with Bella. The woman was self-sufficient and evidently knew where she was going.

Bella raised her dark eyes. They were indomitable and hard as coal. Diane, who had always got on easily with people, found herself at a loss to make further conversation since Bella had no intention of being friends with her. But she made the overture.

'I suppose you find it painful to talk about what has happened to your home,' she said quietly. 'I know I should myself. I would like you to know, though, that anything I can do to help I will only be too happy to do.'

'I appreciate your good intentions,' Bella replied. 'Unfortunately there is nothing that an outsider can do. You do not belong to the Valmardi family, nor are you likely to. How long do you propose to stay here at the Quinta, Miss McNair?'

Diane stared for a long moment at the insolent regard bestowed upon her, and decided to keep her temper and her dignity in the face of insult.

'Until I leave,' she replied calmly. 'I'm sorry that you feel the need to be so offensive. Why are you so afraid of me?'

Bella gave a derisive laugh. 'You flatter yourself, Miss McNair. Why should I be afraid of you? You could not possibly constitute any threat to me, I can assure you.'

'No? But my presence here at the Quinta does. I wonder why?'

The long fingers plucked at the counterpane and Bella drew herself up indignantly.

'Your insolence is only what I can expect. I know of your free and easy ways in England, but we do not tolerate them here. It would be to your advantage to remember that,' she said ominously.

Diane fought back her anger and replaced it with contempt. She said evenly, 'There is nothing wrong in being free and easy providing one does nothing wrong. I came to see you to offer my condolences and any help it might have been in my power to give. However, thank you for clearing the air. At least you and I now know where we stand. Incidentally, I much prefer my own free and easy way to your rather questionable ones—and I didn't care for that last remark either, since it seemed to hold a threat. Not being one of the Valmardi family does have its advantages, *senhorita*, since it leaves me under no obligation to be even polite to you. I will leave you to ponder upon that. Thank you for asking me to sit down.'

With this last sarcastic rejoinder, Diane stalked from the room fuming with anger. Phew, what a woman! One thing was certain—Maria's dislike of the woman was not misplaced.

The Senhora met her as she made her way to her room.

'How is the invalid?' she asked with her charming smile.

'Doing nicely, I would say. Having her home burned down seems to have been the tonic she needed. I shall have to try it myself some time,' Diane said lightly.

The Senhora laughed, a pleasant little tinkle. 'Bella is one of those women who can hide their true feelings. To a girl of your lovely, open disposition, she's hard to understand. And you must remember this,' She lifted a playful finger. 'She must be terribly jealous of you.'

'Jealous of me? You mean of my presence here?'

'That and your beautiful self. You have an inward shining beauty, the beauty of a warm, loving heart, and the sensitive nature that shows you care for everything and everyone around you. I suppose one could call it charm.

My son and daughter both have it because, like you, they're natural in all they say and do. I've often lain awake through the dark hours praying that they might find the right partner. I suppose it comes of having no dear husband to help me. So I live in hope.'

Impulsively, Diane kissed her cheek. 'I don't think you need to fear about Maria. She will never cause you any pain. She adores you. As for your son, he can take care of himself.'

Maria was not in evidence when she reached her room and Diane was thankful for the respite. She touched up her make-up and smoothed down the blue linen sun dress before adding the smart little jacket. The upsetting interlude with Bella had shaken her firm resolve to stay on at the Quinta for Maria's sake. She gazed out into the fresh beauty of a heavenly morning, and her heart seeemed to stop beating as she gazed down at the loveliness of sea and sky with the knowledge that there was a poignancy about it that hurt. The familiar scene, with the lovely curve of the bay, the towering stately trees, the deep golden shadows with the coloured plumage of the birds darting across them seemed to fade into an unreality into which she had intruded.

What would happen now with Bella always there—remorselessly pursuing her objective in the role of a relative claiming naturally certain rights? Diane knew that her own sensitive nature had not the flippant casualness to ignore that presence nor to endure and be reminded continually of her relationship with Alonso. And as she went wearily to seek Maria and learn her wishes for the day, Diane felt that with Bella in the Quinta it was going to be difficult to recreate their old familiarity in the special friendship which existed between them.

Maria, however, appeared normal enough, with plans for a picnic lunch and bathing on one of the secluded warm beaches. The car was sent back to the Quinta de Valmardi with instructions to return to Funchal at five o'clock to take them home. After their picnic lunch they went to

Monte to ride in one of the sledges, allowing a cool breeze to blow on their sunburned cheeks.

Maria cried with delight, 'Can you imagine Bella disporting herself on one of these? I am sure she will drive Alonso mad within a month of their marriage. Not that he would approve of us doing this and joining in with the tourists. Oh, I am glad that you came, Diane! I am just beginning to live,' she chuckled as they sped down the slopes.

But Diane did not echo her delight, and when the golden heat of the day merged into the cooler air of evening, she felt almost a relief at their return to the Quinta. She dressed for dinner that night thoroughly convinced that what Alonso had said about her influencing his sister had been true. It had been done unconsciously by the news of her own activities in her letters over the years. The thought suddenly occurred to her that Maria could end up by refusing to marry Felipe or anyone connected with her own way of life. As she knew that this would upset her family and might not make in the end for Maria's personal happiness, Diane sat down to do a bit of deep thinking.

Dinner that evening was a rather subdued affair with everyone being affected by the tragedy of Bella's *quinta* except that young woman herself. She appeared at dinner looking none the worse for her experience. Alonso, Diane thought, looked a little strained, and after the meal asked Bella and his mother to accompany him to his study.

Maria's lips tightened as she watched them go and she said urgently, 'Let us go out into the garden for a few moments. I do not know about you, but I always feel tired when I have been to Funchal.' She stifled a yawn. 'The moment my head touches the pillow tonight, I shall be fast asleep.'

'Lucky you,' murmured Diane, linking her arm as they strolled out together. Then she added more warily, 'Maria, what would you do if I had to go back home suddenly? I mean, I might have the opportunity of a good job somewhere that I couldn't afford to pass over.'

Maria laughed as they made for the silver tree and sat down. 'Marry Felipe, I suppose, and let Alonso marry his horrid Bella. But you will not think of going home yet, will you?' She sobered suddenly and gripped Diane's hand.

'I'm thinking it's the best thing I can do,' Diane answered.

'But you have not got a new job to go to, so why go now just when we need you?' Maria cried, visibly distressed. 'It is something Bella has said to you. I know you went to see her this morning. Why did you?'

Diane avoided the anxious dark eyes raking her face. 'It was the normal thing to do under the circumstances. I really thought she was ill with the shock of what happened, and you remember how ill she looked when Alonso carried her to the car?'

Maria made a gesture of contempt. 'All pure acting. Do you not see? She knew Alonso was calling to see her. An extra coating of powder on a face already devoid of make-up and the feigned collapse was easy enough. I tell you, you are too nice to realise what a viper that woman can be. Did you see her this evening at dinner? She was as well as you and I.'

Diane did not answer for a moment but folded Maria's hand between her own. It felt very hot to her touch and she reached out a hand to place on her forehead. That was burning too.

She said with compunction, 'You feel feverish, Maria, and you have no wrap. I think it will be wise for us to go indoors. I hope you haven't caught a chill. The sun was very hot and we were steaming when we went up to the cooler air of Monte.'

'But it was such fun,' Maria cried, forgetting for a moment the subject of their conversation. Suddenly she shivered, and Diane, now thoroughly concerned, rose to her feet, pulling Maria up with her.

'Come on, you're going to bed,' she said firmly.

After seeing Maria in bed with a warm drink brought up on her instructions by one of the staff, Diane went thoughtfully to her own room. The other three were still in Alonso's study and she was too tired, to disillusioned to conjecture on the reason for the discussion they were engaged in. At the moment all that concerned her was Maria's temperature which, she was sure, was much above normal. Maybe she was worrying too much and the hot drink with a good night's sleep would leave her feeling normal in the morning. It had been on the tip of her tongue to wait for the Senhora to leave the study and confide her fears to her. Then it occurred to her that Alonso's mother had enough to put up with at the moment without worrying her about something that had every chance of clearing itself up by morning.

She stood for long moments at her window breathing in the sweet smell of eucalyptus mingled with the scent of frangipani and feeling too restless to think of bed. She bit her lip and wondered what to do, then lay fully dressed on her bed to consider it. She yawned once or twice and gradually her eyelids drooped. When she awoke it was dark and she hastily consulted her illuminated travelling clock, to see that it was past midnight. The next moment she was off the bed and hurrying along to Maria's room. To her relief she found her fast asleep, but her forehead was still burning.

Afraid to take any risk, Diane made her way downstairs hoping fervently that Alonso had not gone to bed. The doctor would be calling to see Bella again, so there was no harm in asking Alonso to let him see Maria too. To her relief Alonso was just leaving his study alone when she went downstairs and he saw her as he closed the door behind him in the hall.

Desperately, she said, 'I must speak to you for a moment. I know it's late, but it's very important.'

The dark eyes perused her face swiftly. 'Certainly,' he said. 'Let us return to the study.' He allowed her to precede him and followed her in, placing a chair at her disposal while he looked down at her intently. He had switched on the lights and his dark eyes narrowed at her heightened colour. 'I hope the sun is responsible for your colour,' he remarked dryly. 'Or are you excited about something?'

'A bit of both,' she answered. 'I'm hoping that Maria's colour is due only to the sun as well.'

She went on to tell him of her fears of Maria having caught a chill, and he listened quietly until she had finished. The look on his face when she had finished was not very encouraging.

Icily he said, 'And whose idea was it for you both to go to Monte? Maria knows quite well that I would disapprove of her going there on the sledges. It is the last place a young woman would go who has a regard for decorum.'

Diane was silent, since it was Maria's idea in the first place, and that silence seemed to convince him of her guilt. Since some explanation seemed essential, she said rather huskily, 'I'm sorry I have appeared to influence Maria, but no real harm has been done, and none that I can't put right by going away. I'm sure everything will be as you wish it once I've gone.'

'So you are convinced that once you are gone everything will go back to normal as before. The fire at the *quinta* will never have happened, Maria will marry her intended and I shall be happy also. Is that what you think?'

Her eyes swerved away from the gleam in his as he pushed his hands into his pockets and glared down at her. 'Do you know what I think, indeed what I know? That we shall never recover from your visit—and now I shall go upstairs to satisfy myself as to Maria's condition. You will please come with me and wait outside her door in case two of us entering will awaken her from the sleep she needs.'

Alonso strode across the room and opened the door for her. They crossed the hall together and walked up the stairs in silence. Then he left her at Maria's door while he stole in quietly to assure himself that all was well. He was back again fairly quickly to say in an undertone as he closed the door softly behind him, 'She is asleep, a little flushed but asleep. Content yourself that she is disgustingly healthy and quite strong. You will now go to bed yourself and I will bring you a drink in case you also have hooked a chill on your outing today.'

Before Diane could make any protest as to the need for bringing her a preventative to a chill he was striding back along the deeply carpeted corridor and dropping quickly down the stairs. She waited for him to return before starting to undress and left her door for him to enter in case his deep voice on the corridor penetrated to other bedrooms.

He came in and stood over her while she drank the draught, then took the glass and was gone. The drink must have been fairly potent, for her eyelids drooped when her head touched the pillow and she relaxed into slumber, to be awakened by uneasy dreams. The illuminated hands of her clock told her that it was three o'clock, a very important time of night when a person's illness could take a turn either way. Knowing that another visit to Maria's room was essential before she could sleep through the rest of the night, Diane rose from her bed, pulled on a filmy negligée over her nightie, and without troubling to put on her bedroom mules, she went out into the corridor and crept to Maria's door. The moment she opened the door it was evident that Maria was tossing and turning in her bed. The quiet noises she was making were distressed ones and she was pushing her head wildly back into her pillow.

Diane gently pushed the heavy black hair from the hot forehead and held one of her hot hands. The dark eyes fluttered open at her touch, but there was no recognition in them. Diane shivered, then turned startled as someone entered the room. It was Alonso. He wore a velvet smoking jacket over his slacks with a silk scarf tucked in at the neck. It was perfectly obvious that he had not been to bed. At first, his look was as startled as her own and she realised in horror that her gossamer negligée, while suitable to be worn in the privacy of her rooms, was hardly the kind of thing in which to confront a man as fastidious as the Duque de Valmardi.

Her legs felt as though they did not belong to her as she rose slowly to her feet.

'I'm—so glad you—you've come,' she stammered in embarrassment. 'Maria is much worse. You should send for the doctor. She's delirious.'

'I know,' he answered. His features were once more enigmatic, his manner formal. 'The doctor was sent for hours ago, but he was out on a case. However, I believe he is now on his way here. You had better go to bed quickly before he arrives.'

The dark eyes sliding over her slim figure in the offending negligée added more weight than words could have conveyed. But Diane was weeping unrestrainedly, and brushing the tears away from a pale downcast face. Alonso appeared to be taken aback by the tears and his smile was kindly.

'Do not upset yourself about Maria. There are many wonderful drugs today that will stem almost any illness. Please go to bed.'

Childishly, Diane drew the tips of her fingers across her cheeks to remove the tears, bit her lip to stop it quivering and went quickly from the room. She was awake for a long time and was not asleep when someone entered the room. Her heart dipped as she sensed Alonso's presence, and she pushed herself up in bed as he switched on the wall lights and came nearer to the bed.

'The doctor has just gone,' he said quietly. 'He has diagnosed a form of meningism which could lead to meningitis if not checked. Fortunately he is confident that he can do something about it before any harm is done. Maria is asleep and, according to the doctor, will be much improved in the morning. However, I propose to sit with her during the night in order to see that the doctor's instructions are carried out.'

'Thank you for coming to tell me,' she said huskily. 'I hope the Senhora is not too upset.'

'Mother has not been told. I saw no reason to do so now that the doctor has the matter in hand. Tomorrow will be soon enough for her to know. I will leave you now to get some sleep. *Boa noite*, Diane. Sleep well.'

When he had gone Diane slid down into bed, realising how upset he must have been himself. He was very much attached to Maria and all that time waiting for the doctor to come must surely have been purgatory for him. But he had borne it alone, preferring not to disturb his mother and cause her anguish. First Bella, then Maria. Poor Alonso! She would have given anything to have been able to sit with him during those hours of anguish and speak words of comfort. But it was not words of comfort from Diane McNair that he wanted. Diane buried her face into her pillow.

CHAPTER NINE

Diane had overslept and was awakened by Sofia entering, bringing with her the pleasant aroma of fresh coffee from the tray she carried.

'The Senhor Duque gave instructions not to waken you, miss,' she said with a smile as Diane pushed herself up in bed to receive the tray. 'He also wishes you to know that Senhorita Maria is much better this morning and he suggests you going in to see her when she has rested after lunch. A nurse has been installed, but it will only be a matter of days before the Senhorita is up and about again. We all are very happy to know that all will be well.'

Diane breathed an inward sigh of relief. 'Have you seen the Senhora this morning? I hope she was not too upset?' she said, lifting up the coffee pot.

'The Senhora is quite well. She went out after breakfast when the doctor had called with the Senhor Duque and Senhorita Vangroot.' Sofia went to the window to draw aside the curtains and spoke over her shoulder. 'I did not bring you much breakfast because lunch is only a matter of an hour or so away. I will bring you more if you want it.'

Diane looked down at the crisp brown rolls, the wads of golden butter, the cherry jam, honey and dish of fruit and knew that she had never felt less like eating.

'This will do fine, thanks,' she answered, drinking her coffee as Sofia left the room. She could not eat any of the breakfast, though, and put a hand to her aching head. Lying in bed so late had never suited her. It had always left her with a heavy head. This morning was no exception. She dressed lethargically in the first thing that came to hand in the wardrobe, a blue and white check sun dress with a square bodice and tailored skirt. She mused wryly that headaches could be cured. It was the dull pain in her

161

heart that was incurable. It was something she had to live with, this intolerable ache for Alonso which she knew he would never fill because he loved another. Diane could not recognise herself as the girl who had come out so joyfully to meet her pen-friend of many years' standing. She had tried to picture Alonso as the brother of Maria, but had never in her wildest dreams imagined that he would eventually mean her whole life, the very pivot of her own existence. How then could she ever let him go to walk through life without him?

It was just before lunch that she went into the garden, hoping for the fresh air to clear her throbbing temples. The edges of the lawns were mottled with shadow and colour from the profusion of flowers which abounded. The hibiscus was especially beautiful this morning, spreading forth with a reckless splendour the beauty of their bell-like blossoms, peach-coloured with dark scarlet centres. Near the silver tree other hibiscus shrubs of many colours blazed against the bougainvillaea. But it was the scent of eucalyptus which Diane breathed in to great depth which seemed to ease the pain in her head.

On her return to the Quinta the sound of a car arriving heralded what she took to be Alonso, his mother and Bella arriving. But to her surprise and joy it was Felipe who strode towards her.

'Felipe!' she cried, taking his hand warmly in her own. 'What a pleasant surprise! You've come to see Maria, of course?'

Felipe greeted her with his usual courteous restrained manner, but she felt a slight tremor in his hand as he drew the other wretchedly across his blond hair. His face was pale and grim, his voice thickening as he spoke.

'How is Maria?' he asked. 'Alonso explained to me the nature of her illness and I came as quickly as I could. She is not going to die, is she?'

Diane gave a small reassuring laugh. 'Goodness, no! She is definitely out of danger. The illness was caught in time and she'll soon be up and about again. Alonso's instructions are for me to go and see her when she's rested after lunch—which means that you can lunch with me and go in to see her later.' She smiled up at him, linking her arm in his as they walked into the Quinta. 'I'd like to bet that you have had nothing to eat since you had the news about Maria.'

He shrugged broad shoulders. 'How is one expected to eat at a time like this? If Maria were to ...'

Words failed him, and Diane squeezed his arm. 'Food is what you need at the moment. Going without it isn't going to solve a thing, so you're going to eat a good lunch.'

During the meal Diane encouraged Felipe to talk. He had great plans for expanding the wine making and the agricultural side of the estate. In a world of an evergrowing population there was an increasing demand for food and drink, so he could not go wrong in a plan of expansion. Diane listened with a kind of approval mixed with envy. Felipe might be losing in matters of the heart, but he certainly knew where he was going.

The look of strain left his face and Diane felt a measure of satisfaction in having helped to erase it. It was three o'clock when she suggested that he went to see Maria. He drew a hand over his hair again and looked wretched.

'You are coming with me? You have seen how Maria has treated me of late—as if she could not bear the sight of me. With you there she is sure to welcome us.'

Diane hesitated. 'But, Felipe, don't you think you have a right to go to see her whenever you choose as her intended? It seems to me that it's time that you took a firmer line with that young woman,' she said firmly.

He rose to his feet. 'Strange that you should mention that,' he said heavily. 'I have been thinking about it—but now is not the time. Maria will be in no fit state to decide anything at the moment. Shall we go?'

Rather unwillingly Diane went with him out of the *sala* and into the hall. What he had said was right, she thought, but his approach was all wrong. Now Alonso, she was sure, would behave very differently. He would not have entertained any argument from Maria as to their betrothal, but would have swept her off her feet. Few girls could resist caveman tactics, and that was what she had to get through to Felipe if he was to win Maria. She thought of Alonso as a lover, found it too hurtful, and stared with amazement to see him coming into the Quinta accompanied by his mother and Bella.

His dark eyes dwelt on the two of them for an enigmatic minute, then he was striding forward delightedly with his white smile to greet Felipe.

'So you managed to come,' he cried cordially. 'Have you seen Maria?'

'We were on our way to her room now,' Felipe replied. His regard for Alonso was fond and Diane sensed a bond between them which many brothers would have envied. It occurred to her then what a close-knit group they were. She could see why Alonso insisted upon his sister marrying Felipe so as to pave the way for his own marriage to Bella. That way there would be no problems. Everything would go on as before and Diane McNair would soon be forgotten. She clenched her hands by her sides and felt the pain again in her temples. Bella was looking at her curiously, but the Senhora was smiling warmly. Only Alonso was raking her face with hard glittering dark eyes.

'We must not delay you, Felipe,' he said with a dangerous calm. 'I am sure you are eager to see Maria. You know, of course, that all danger has passed and that she will soon be well again?'

'Diane has already told me,' he replied. 'She has been a great comfort.'

Gravely, yet with a trace of mockery, Alonso's eyes were once again on Diane's pale face.

'I am sure she has,' he said tersely. 'Diane's influence can be quite something when she sets her mind to it, as Maria will no doubt tell you. Maria regards her as a sister. I shall be in my study when you come down again, Felipe.' A pause, then, 'You have had lunch?'

Felipe nodded, inclined his head in greeting to the Senhora, and asked how she was. Then after repeating the procedure with Bella he turned to take the stairs two at a time after a meaning glance at Diane, who was prevented from following him by Alonso's hand on her arm. He waited until the Senñora and Bella had moved towards the *sala* before he spoke.

'That look just now that you exchanged with Felipe,' he said curtly, 'please define it.' His voice was low and savage. His hold tightened and Diane looked at him in startled amazement. His dark eyes glittered, his nostrils distended and she felt sure he was going to do her an injury.

'You're hurting my arm,' she protested.

Thin-lipped, he slackened his hold but did not fully release her.

'I am waiting,' he said.

'For what?' Diane was deliberately obtuse. How dared he take such a high-handed attitude with her? And whatever had got into him? She trembled, not with fear, but with the thrill of blood running through her veins like fire at his touch.

'What is Felipe to you?' he insisted.

For some time Diane was incapable of movement or speech. All she could do was to stare up at the arrogant demand in the dark eyes. Then her anger flared to meet his.

'I find your attitude rather insulting,' she flared. 'What could there possibly be between Felipe and me except friendship?'

A dark eyebrow shot up in disbelief. 'Is that not a well-known expression frequently used by the English when contradicting any hint of an alliance between two people, that they are just good friend?'

Diane shrugged slim shoulders. Her tones icy, she said, 'I am not in the habit of making up to the boy-friend of a good friend. Needless to say, Felipe is also one of my best friends on the island, so make what you will of that!'

His eyes narrowed dangerously. Then he became very much the Duque, restrained and courteous.

With less curtness, he said, 'I am aware that you came to us at a most unfortunate time, and if I have seemed to be unfriendly, I am sorry. However, the time will come when you will cease taking a back seat, as it were, and begin to be our honoured guest. Until that time comes I ask you to keep an open mind about what is happening here at the Quinta. I am not at liberty to tell you more now.'

Diane stood perfectly still as the nature of his remarks got through to her. Of course, she would be the honoured guest when Maria married and when he married too, only she could not wait that long. She had already suffered enough at the hands of this dark-eyed autocrat who expected her to dance at his wedding as she would at Maria's.

'I have no wish to comment,' she answered with a youthful dignity which, had she but known it, made her look vulnerable and very young. 'I'm going to my room now. Perhaps you'll be good enough to let me know when it's convenient for me to see Maria.' She looked down at his hand on her arm and added, 'Now, if you'll be good enough to release me ...'

But he retained his hold. 'I will not have Maria upset by you telling her of your departure, you understand? You will stay until she is better. By then you might be in a more sensible frame of mind.'

'Upset her? I upset her? You must be joking!' Looking up into his dark compelling face, Diane wanted to hurt him and go on hurting just as the hand resting with a deceptive lightness on her arm was hurting right through her being to her heart. 'You're the right one to talk when you're hurting her more than anyone ever could!'

Was it her imagination or was it a trick of the light? Diane could not be sure, but it seemed to her that he had gone paler and it suddenly struck her that he looked tired. After all, he had been up all night sitting with Maria, but there was an air about him almost of desperation. Diane felt suddenly ashamed of her outburst. After all, if he loved Bella, who was she, or anyone else for that matter, to deny him his love? As for Maria, marriage would take her away

166

from any contact with her brother's wife, and she was sure that it was only a matter of time before she decided to marry Felipe.

For a long moment she stared up into the dark eyes as his hand dropped from her arm. Then he said very quietly, 'I was hoping . . .' He paused and he seemed to reach some decision. 'I will see you in my study this evening at six o'clock.'

The next moment he turned on his heel and left her. Diane went slowly up to her room, her nerves still tingling, her head aching. In her room she did not feel much better. Unable to sit down, she paced the room wondering what it was that Alonso wanted to see her about. The only possible answer was that he was going to ask her to leave. Maybe he was hoping that Felipe would come to some arrangement with Maria, thus leaving her free to go back to London. Well, anything was better than staying on to be tortured by Alonso's presence.

She walked to the window to look out at the mountains, as placid and immovable as they had been for generations, and recalled the huge eucalyptus tree down below in the garden from which Alonso had plucked a leaf for her to savour the perfume. That same leaf was now tucked away between the pages of one of her paperback books in her case. That and the wristwatch he had given her were the only mementoes of her stay in Madeira.

For Diane, leaving the island would give a sharp pang of unbelievable pain. She would miss the glittering jagged edges of the mountains piercing the blue skies, the sweet-scented breezes and velvet nights, the hot cobblestones, the sledges, and the leisurely way of life adding to the delights of Funchal, the respectful greetings of the people and the astonishing lovely gardens of the Quinta de Valmardi. An impending sense of fatality was taking possession of her senses, bring with it an inner sense of confusion which she felt powerless to resist.

Her thoughts turned to Maria, her sweet, sisterly affection, the Senhora who had shown such warm interest in her comings and goings, Felipe, shy, kind, and filled with unhappiness—and to Alonso. She saw the years ahead haunted by the thoughts of him sharing his life with his wife, living with her in this gracious house, sharing his bed in one of the lovely rooms looking out on a view similar to the one she now gazed upon. Looking down on the quiet garden, pale as the magnolia blossom that hung in such white soft luxury over the lawns, Diane again remembered his magnetism. The memory of his dark face brought an agony of joy to her darkened world and she put her hands up to her face in an attempt to forget him.

When a soft tap on her door brought her back to the present, Diane hastily pulled herself together and with an attempt to sound cheerful bade whoever it was to come in. To her surprise Bella entered and closed the door softly. Her dark, secretive eyes flickered; she smiled the dangerous and enigmatic smile which, Diane mused, could interest men but which to her held hidden depths.

Diane looked at her making no attempt to hide her surprise, but was wise enough to keep silent.

'I trust that I am not disturbing you,' Bella said composedly, as she came into the room. 'I would like a word with you in private.' The dark eyes were intent upon Diane's face. 'If it is convenient.'

'Sit down.' Diane gestured to a chair but remained standing herself. To her the meeting was not friendly enough for her to sit down and chat, so she leaned back against the dressing table and waited.

Bella sat down and smoothed her dress. 'I want to ask you a favour,' she began carefully.

Diane looked at her in astonishment. 'You want to ask a favour of me? I find that hard to believe, knowing how you dislike me.' Her lips felt stiff, immobile. 'Why me?'

'Because you are the only one I can ask. I am perfectly aware that Maria does not like me, nor the Senhora. I would like to go back to my *quinta* to salvage a few things —personal belongings, you understand? Alonso has forbidden me to return, says it is not safe, but I know my rooms are not that much damaged. If you come with me no comment will be made. I can leave word that we have gone out for a drive ... please, Miss McNair.'

A strange feeling of unease made Diane hesitate. Her throat felt dry. The Quinta was very quiet, and Bella watched her, speculative, intent. Her voice continued, her full red lips forming words honey-sweet.

'I know that you and I have not been friends, but I know that you are to be trusted. That is most important to me. I saw a member of my staff in Funchal this morning and he is coming to pick me up in ten minutes here to take me to my *quinta*.'

Diane frowned. 'You mean you went to Funchal this morning? I thought you were out with Senhora de Valmardi and her son?'

'I was,' smoothly. 'We had some business to attend to. I managed to have a word with Carlos unobserved. He is still in my employ. All my staff are.'

'But your personal maid? Why not take her with you? Why me? Why do you want me to come?'

Bella said evenly, 'I do not want you to come, not specially, but I have no choice.' The full red lips twisted into a secret and not quite pleasant smile. The honeyed tones hardened a little. The dark eyes were hard again as though tired of keeping up the mask of friendliness. 'I do not want anyone here at the Quinta de Valmardi to know where I have gone, for Alonso would most certainly prevent me. As I have said, going with you would arouse no suspicion and I trust you. Is that not reason enough?'

Diane hesitated. She thought, I'm behaving as though I was afraid of her. Why should I be? A drive to the blackened *quinta* would be a break before dinner that evening and probably no one would know that they had been. Besides, Bella could not be all that bad if Alonso loved her. There could be a human streak which the woman kept hidden from all eyes, and she had suffered quite a bit of misfortune with her father leaving her in such dire straits. The woman might want to be friends, and she could meet her half way.

'Very well. If it's as you say I will go with you. We

shall be back for dinner?' Diane spoke with a friendly warmth. She even managed a faint friendly smile, but her heart was beating fast as she straightened from the dressing table. 'I take it we go now?'

Bella rose to her feet with a smile of satisfaction. 'As quickly as possible,' she said.

The car was parked a considerable distance from the Quinta along the drive. Bella went forward quickly to speak in an undertone to the driver, who replied in guttural tones and eyed Diane sullenly as he assisted them into the car. At Bella's suggestion both girls sat in the back, but Diane would have preferred Bella to sit in front with the driver to give her time to clarify her uneasiness into something calmer and more normal. They had met no one on their way out of the Quinta to the car, and the idea that Bella had timed their leaving in order that they would not be seen was not to be dismissed lightly. Then a degree of reasonableness prevailed and she chided herself for being an idiot. In a way it was a relief to get away from the Quinta for a while.

The car slid away from the first pair of double gates to the drive and was soon going in between the second pair, which were open. Bella was not inclined to talk and Diane gave herself up to the scenery and the joy of the delights of nature. The car was purring through the hills along incredibly winding roads through eucalyptus, olive trees and pines. Diane was thinking of Alonso, who had driven along this same road many times with Bella. He had probably talked to her in that teasing, charming way he had with everyone but herself, and might even have stopped to kiss her in the shade of the Madeira laurels now lining the road. But the scenery was too interesting to allow tortuous thoughts to prevail, especially with frangipani filling the air with its intoxicating scent.

Diane found her second visit to the blackened shell of Bella's *quinta* to be more forbidding than the first. The broken roof towered like a broken mass of mountain above the gracefully spaced wings, unsafe and filled with menace.

170

She suppressed a shiver as they left the car. Bella hung back to speak a few hurried words to the driver, who drove away as she returned to Diane's side.

'Carlos is calling for us later,' she explained, and they entered the hall.

A slight draught blew across Diane's face from the tall windows now broken by the heat of the fire. The expensive rugs on the hall floor were grimy and smoke-blackened, but the grand staircase was intact. No members of the staff came forward to greet them and Diane wondered if the place was as deserted as it appeared to be. A dread feeling of crisis dried her throat as they crossed the hall.

Bella said forcefully, 'I want to go to my rooms to collect some things. No one would believe that there had been a fire in that wing of the *quinta*. It seemed to have escaped, but most of the other rooms are ruined.'

Diane spoke mechanically, her head back, her eyes looking up to the high raftered roof meandering into shadow.

'Alonso said something about the fire having started in the kitchen regions. That would account for the other wing remaining intact.'

Bella agreed eagerly to this and Diane could see a sense of excitement darkening the brown eyes as she caught her arm.

'Let us go down to investigate,' she said, pulling Diane across the hall to a door at the side of the staircase. 'I was too upset on the day of the fire to do anything about it.'

Bella opened the door to a corridor, but Diane hung back, strangely reluctant to enter the burned-out part of the *quinta*. An arid smell of stale smoke and damp from the firemen's hoses struck her nostrils, and Bella's look, an almost fanatical gleam lighting her dark eyes, frightened her.

'Do you think it wise to go into this part of the building? Surely it isn't safe to prowl around?' she queried.

But Bella was propelling her forward along the corridor. The kitchen was a blackened shell with a huge hole in the ceiling showing right through to the rooms above and con-

171

tinuing to the caved-in roof. The lovely tiled walls of the kitchen were cracked and broken and the huge fireplace was a large gaping hole.

Diane gazed around and felt an urge to be gone. 'How terrible!' she exclaimed with a tremor in her voice. 'The place is completely burned out. It must have had quite a hold when the fire brigade arrived.' She shuddered. 'It's lucky you weren't all burned in your beds.'

Bella, who was looking around the room with her eyes as if searching for something, answered with her thoughts obviously elsewhere.

'The staff were away at the church fair in the village. I was alone in my room when I smelled the burning. I—I was sick of being alone—alone in a place that I could not keep going in the way I wanted. A Portuguese woman brought up as I was to appreciate the finer arts and a gracious way of living has to have a husband, and what could I do?' She beat one fist into the palm of her other hand fiercely. 'I had had proposals, but they were from suitors almost as impoverished as myself.'

Diane put a hand on her shoulder in a gesture of compassion. 'I'm sorry,' she said gently. 'But surely possessions aren't everything. Surely love comes first?'

'Love!' The dark eyes blazed as Bella almost spat out the word. Her lips were twisted with scorn. 'How much does love count when one's whole life is at stake, one's social standing? Do you think I could have been happy with the peasants in the fields? I, Bella Vangroot, who can trace back my family for generations? And if I had not had enough to contend with the whole thing, all my plans began to mock at me when you arrived, with your English colouring, your feminine wiles, and your determination to trap Alonso, my Alonso, into marriage. Deny it if you can!'

Diane dropped her hand from the now trembling shoulder. 'You're wrong,' she said, her eyes wide with horror and dismay. She was doing quite a bit of trembling herself. 'Alonso has never liked me—he told me so. In fact I was going to end my visit soon. You have nothing to fear from me.'

'You cannot deny that you love him. I have seen that look in your eyes whenever he is near. I know that kind of look well enough, for I have had it myself.' The dark eyes, hard and determined, held hers. The air was suddenly chill as for a moment they eyed one another. Accusation, denial. Diane held her breath. 'Do you take me for a fool?' Bella hissed.

Diane shook her head dazedly. 'Listen to me, Bella.' She held out slender hands, rosy-tipped, and smiled tenderly. 'If Alonso loves you then there's nothing for you to torment yourself with. You brought me here to tell me all this, didn't you? You say you are no fool, then stop behaving like one and collect what you came for. This place gives me the creeps. I don't think we ought to be here. Let's go.'

Between the dark lashes the dark eyes gleamed, and the teeth showed in a smile which was no smile.

'You would have me believe that I was wrong about you despite the evidence of my own eyes?' Bella demanded. 'This look you gave Alonso was because of your sisterly love for him, because Maria was like a sister to you? Is that what you would have me believe?'

Diane lifted her chin and answered honestly, 'I love Alonso, Maria and the Senhora—who wouldn't? You must be fond of them yourself. They've been so kind to you.'

Bella's eyes were impersonal again, her mouth serene. 'I will take your word for it,' she conceded. 'And to show that there is no ill feeling I will take you to the rooms where I played as a child. Come.'

Diane, shaken by Bella's sudden change of mood, was immediately suspicious. 'Where are these rooms?' she asked, then brightened. 'I know, you've come to collect some of your treasures from them. I hope you haven't lost them all.'

'That remains to be seen,' Bella said darkly, and they left the kitchen to walk along the corridor into the hall. Diane walked lightly beside her. The great empty shell of the *quinta* was only a temporary menace. Her spirits lifted.

They made their way upstairs. Half way up the stairs branched off into two separate flights with the stairs to the right leading to the wing untouched by fire, Bella's own rooms. To Diane's surprise and dismay, Bella's close grip on her arm turned her to the stairs leading to the damaged wing of the house. Uneasily she shot a glance at Bella's closed profile, then decided to humour her and hope for the best. Cool draughts of air greeted them when they reached the corridor from a ceiling open in parts to the sky. Diane shivered as they passed doors off their hinges leading into fire-damaged rooms. Bella, perfectly composed, paused at a door half way along the corridor which was in better shape than the others and opened it.

'This is the nursery,' she said. 'In the cupboards under the window seats you will find some of my childhood treasures. Will you collect them for me and bring them to my rooms in the west wing?'

Diane nodded and entered the room. Across the room tall windows were hung with what was left of velvet curtains. Below them the window seats and cupboards appeared to be nursery furniture. Diane walked across what had once been a valuable Chinese carpet—and suddenly the floor became hinged as in an earthquake. Too late she realised that part of the floor had gone and the carpet placed cunningly over the hole. She tried to draw back and found herself slipping down—down into blackness. Something struck her head and the carpet wrapped around her suffocatingly.

She opened her eyes to find that her nose and mouth were filled with dust. The carpet was swathed around her like a cocoon and she realised that it had probably saved her life by cushioning her against the fall through to the ground floor of the *quinta*. Her head was throbbing violently and the dust irritated her nose and throat painfully. She began cough and each spasm sent knife-thrusts of pain to her temples. When the coughing ceased Diane found that the carpet had formed a funnel above her head through which she could see the sky. Moving gingerly, she tried to wriggle herself out of the heavy folds, but it was hard going. She was virtually a prisoner, hemmed in by debris, with no idea how long she had been there. Her confused guess was that some piece of furniture in the nursery had been dislodged and had fallen through the hole in the floor, hitting her head as it fell and knocking her out.

Common sense warned her against shouting for help since the vibration of her voice might loosen other furniture or debris poised precariously on the brink of broken floors above her, and bring it down. Weak tears stung her eyes as she thought of Bella. Where was she? Was it possible that she had placed the carpet as a trap and left her to her fate? Had she returned to the nursery, seen the gaping hole in the floor, waited for Carlos to return, then had told him that the English *senhorita* had already left in a friend's car? Or had she been devious enough to dash out to him the moment he had arrived to go back with him to the Quinta de Valmardi in order to get help for Diane who was lost in the ruins of the building? The second story would be more probable, since Bella could deny all knowledge of the nursery floor being unsafe. Alonso would believe her, of course.

Thoughts ran around in her aching head like a demented hornet. If Bella had planned the accident, why? Was it jealousy? If only the woman knew what little cause she had to be jealous! Perhaps the shock of the fire had deranged her temporarily and she had gone berserk. It could happen. The thing was, Diane had to get herself out. She tried to move again and managed to free her arms. Now if she could pull herself up far enough to reach for the top edge of the carpet above her head, it might be possible for her to lever herself out. No bones appeared to be broken, for she could wiggle her toes and flex her arms freely. It took a long time to wriggle up far enough and beads of perspiration ran down her pale forehead, but with a sick feeling of being bruised and battered she finally made it. But her ordeal was far from over. Debris hung above and around her precariously, most of it having followed her down when she fell. It was a miracle that she had not been seriously injured.

Slowly she pulled the carpet down and levered herself up in doing so. At last only her legs remained below, and right in front of her was a gap in the debris through which she could crawl out. At last, choking and coughing with the dust, Diane staggered up and stumbled out into the lovely scented air of flowers beneath a clear blue sky. She was gulping in deep breaths of air when she heard the car, and gazed furtively around the gable end of the *quinta*.

Alonso was getting quickly out of the car, turning a dark handsome face, ravaged and strained, at the *quinta*. Instinctively, almost without being aware of it, Diane ran to meet him as though obeying some magnetic pull of the heart. When she reached him she was beyond words. Then his hands were gripping her shoulders with a fierce intensity, she trembled violently as she collapsed with her sweet slender suppleness pressed against him. Time stood still while she tried to puzzle out whether or not the powerful beating of her heart was not being subsidised by his. She had forgotten that he was the Duque de Valmardi and that she was merely Diane McNair whom he despised.

Maybe the blow on her head was responsible for her imagining that his arms were tightening around her quivering body, and that he was holding her as though he would never let her go. His lips touched her hair and he seemed visibly moved as he murmured something in Portuguese which seemed to come from the very depths of his being. It was a dream, of course. It simply could not be real. But it was sufficient to know that she was drowning in a sea of bliss not unmixed with despair. These precious moments stolen from time were hers. The rest would belong to Bella. Soon Alonso would take her back to the Quinta de Valmardi where Bella would be waiting to chide her for being so foolish as to stray into danger. And Alonso would believe Bella.

'You are hurt, *pequena*?' His fingers gently moving over the back of her head had stopped short at the place where she had been struck. His swift indrawn breath on finding his fingers sticky with blood was balm for her heart. Her face was buried in his chest and she was glad of his suffocating hold, for she needed his support. Her limbs were throbbing painfully, hammers were going in her head, and her knees were going weak as reaction set in. The next moment she passed out.

When Diane opened her eyes again she was in bed at the

Quinta de Valmardi. She had been wandering in a kind of shadowed dream where someone had kept prodding her gently and apparently taking a fiendish delight in finding all the vulnerable spots which gave her most pain. There had been several needle pricks—or had it merely been nerves twitching? Everything had been so hazy that she could not be sure. There was a bandage on her head and the room smelt of antiseptic dressings.

Everything was hazy, including the tall figure often standing beside her bed to lay the backs of cool fingers against her hot brow. She thought it could be Alonso—but the effort to concentrate was too much. It was far easier to drift into sleep.

On the second day Diane was feeling more herself. Her head felt better and the bruises on her body were not as sore. An adhesive plaster covered the small wound in the back of her head and she had been ordered to stay in bed another day by the doctor. The Senhora came, and Felipe, to ask how she was, and Alonso looked in for brief moments, she noticed, only when someone else was there. He never failed to arrive whenever Felipe came, and he would regard her intently from dark disturbing eyes and ask politely how she was feeling.

Of course, Diane understood why Alonso acted in this way. He only wished to save her and himself embarrassment. That blow on the head had certainly made her imagine things. That time at Bella's *quinta*, for instance, when she had run into his arms. She must have been light in the head to imagine that he had kissed her hair and murmured endearments. When visitors came Diane would whip up moments of spurious gaiety which soon faded when she was alone, leaving her looking pale and pinched.

Maria came in to see her on the second day, looking very much better herself. She made a joke about them sharing the same nurse and was curious as to why Diane should have gone with Bella to her *quinta*. Nothing had been mentioned about it until now and Diane was determined to make light of it. She loved Alonso too much to risk causing him any hurt over Bella; besides, it might not be true that Bella had deliberately planned the accident. Fortunately Senhora de Valmardi came in at that moment and Diane was saved an explanation.

But the following morning when Maria came into her room after breakfast to find her up and dressed, she broached the subject of Bella again.

Diane shrugged. 'Bella asked me to go to her *quinta* with her to pick up some cherished possessions,' she said. 'Trust me to go into a room that wasn't safe!'

She was sitting by the window and Maria had perched on the arm of her chair, looking maternal.

'But surely Bella would know which rooms were safe?' she exclaimed indignantly. 'In any case, she had no right to ask you to go with her. Thank goodness she is not here. Good riddance!'

Diane turned wide eyes in her direction. 'You mean she's left?'

It was Maria's turn to shrug. 'She is not here, which is all I care about. And I am so happy to see you so much better. Do you feel up to a stroll in the garden?'

'That makes two of us,' Diane replied. 'Your recovery has been amazingly swift.'

'Drugs can work miracles these days. Let us go, two old crocks supporting each other.'

They chuckled as they went downstairs together arm in arm to sit under the silver tree.

They talked happily together until Maria said carelessly, 'Felipe goes back to his *quinta* today. He will be out shortly to say goodbye. Alonso ought not to have told him about me. Nothing is settled between us.'

Diane heaved a deep sigh and looked into her friend's obstinate little face.

'Oh dear,' she cried. 'I know you love him. Couldn't you bring yourself to give him some hope? He is so nice, and I'm sure you will regret being so beastly to him.'

Telltale colour swept beneath the magnolia skin as Maria

178

turned her head away. 'I would rather not discuss it, Diane,' she said miserably.

Diane was silent for a while, then she said slowly, 'I don't think Alonso's friendship with Bella has everything to do with the way you treat Felipe. You want something more romantic than just drifting into marriage with someone you've known practically all your life. Now if Felipe had swept you up on his horse that day instead of that awful young man, you would be married to him by now. Come on, admit it. I'm right, aren't I?'

Maria moved uneasily. 'I am not sure how I feel about Felipe,' she answered irritably. 'Oh dear, why does life have to be so—so unexciting?'

Diane said firmly, 'I think Felipe is exciting. I don't know what you want . . .' She broke off to see Felipe coming across the lawn towards them. 'Here is Felipe now. Be nice to him, Maria. Please!'

But Maria did not answer. Rising to her feet, she went swiftly across the lawn, passing an astonished Felipe, and entered the Quinta.

'What is the matter with Maria?' he asked. 'Is she avoiding me?'

Felipe lowered himself into the seat vacated by Maria, stretched out long legs and stared down at them morosely.

Diane's voice was placating. 'Maria is pining for someone to come along on a horse and kidnap her. My guess is that she loves you but is too proud to admit it. Now if you were to make up her mind for her . . .'

Felipe looked at her in utter amazement. 'Are you suggesting that I kidnap Maria on a horse? Why,' he spread out his hands helplessly, 'it is fantastic!'

'It has happened,' Diane told him dryly. 'As a matter of fact it happened right here in these grounds. One of Maria's ancestors rode along the tree-lined road over there and sweeping up his lady love carried her to the lodge in the woods. There she was kept a prisoner until she promised to marry him. I'm not suggesting that you do that, but you

179

could take her to your house and use the same tactics. Maria will love it.'

Felipe was grinning now at secret thoughts. 'It sounds interesting. But would it work? And what about the time and the place?'

'Easy. We shall be here in the garden after lunch. At four o'clock I shall suggest that Maria and I stroll along the road, and the rest is up to you.'.

Felipe looked doubtful. 'I hope it will work.'

'Why not try it and see? What have you got to lose? Cheer up.' Diane laughed and patted his arm. 'If Maria won't have you I will!'

Suddenly he was grinning again. 'That should be an incentive if anything is. In this venture I am your man.'

Demurely she corrected him, 'You will be Maria's man before the day is out. That I promise you.'

CHAPTER TEN

It was all over. Everything had gone according to plan. Diane and Maria had rested after lunch and then gone in the garden to be on sun-loungers. Precisely at four o'clock Diane suggested a stroll along the road leading to the lodge and Maria had agreed. She had been very quiet and thoughtful during lunch, and like Diane, had not had much appetite. Diane could sympathise with her feeling of being under par, for she felt the same herself, and Maria was still recovering from her recent illness. The last thought gave her qualms about Felipe, and these qualms increased as they strolled along the road to hear Felipe trotting behind them. Then everything had happened at once. Maria had been swept from her side, she had a glimpse of a grinning Felipe, and they were gone.

For Diane, standing there and watching them go, it was a kind of anti-climax, something that had to happen to mark the end of her visit to the island. She felt terribly alone as she walked back to the Quinta. The Senhora de Valmardi was out for the day visiting friends and was not expected back until late that night. Alonso was also out. There was nothing for it now except pack her things and make her arrangements for leaving. If things worked out with Maria and Felipe, and it was quite possible that they would, then she would leave with Alonso's blessing.

Diane wondered disconsolately whether he was with Bella at that moment. He had been away from the Quinta for most of the time since he had brought her back on that fatal day from the ruins of Bella's home. Her meals had been taken in her room, but the nurse had left that morning and it was expected that she would dine downstairs that evening for the first time. Her heart trembled at the thought that Alonso and Bella might be there. The whereabouts of

181

Bella were still a mystery, and Diane was still curious as to why Alonso had not questioned her about their visit to the ruined *quinta*. If only she could go away with the knowledge that Alonso would be happily married to Bella, as happy as Maria and Felipe would assuredly be. There was no doubt as to the success of their future. They were meant for each other, two of a kind who would be complete as a whole together. Such happiness was not for herself, for there would never be another man in the whole world whom she could love like Alonso.

Returning to her room, Diane packed most of her things and put the case away to avoid awkward questions when Sofia came in. She wanted to do everything in her own good time with the minimum of fuss, and be able to steal away at the end. The silk jersey dress in warm amber was chosen to give her face a little colour and to boost her morale when she went down to dinner.

Sofia came in as she slipped the dress from the hanger. Agitatedly, she said. 'The Senhorita Maria is not in her room. It is most curious. No one has seen her and the Senhora cannot be consulted because she is out. The Senhor Duque has returned and he wishes to see you, miss, as soon as you are ready.'

Diane allowed Sofia to take the dress and help her into it. Then she said carefully, 'Have you told the Senhor Duque that you can't find the Senhorita Maria?'

Sofia shook her head and shrugged. 'The Senhorita often plays tricks. Who knows? She might be in her room when I return.'

Heaven forbid, thought Diane. 'It is possible that the Senhorita Maria has accompanied Senhor Felipe Moltardo to his house. That is all I can say at the moment.' She paused, then added, 'Have you any idea how many there will be for dinner this evening?'

Sofia answered without hesitation. 'There will be three for dinner, miss. That is all I know.'

Diane went cold inside. Sofia chatted on, complimenting her on her choice of the amber dress so charming against the smooth peach bloom of her tan, but Diane hardly listened. Three for dinner could only mean someone else with Alonso and herself. Was that third person Maria, or Bella? Her first reaction was to tell Sofia that she would prefer a tray to be sent up to her room in lieu of dinner downstairs. Then common sense prevailed over her rising panic. After all, she was leaving the next day. Surely there was some inner reserve of strength she could summon to carry her through her last evening at the Quinta with dignity? And besides, poor Sofia was bemused already. It was hardly fair to involve her further. The right thing to do was to behave normally, and if Bella happened to be there, to call her bluff by going along with anything she said, for Alonso's sake. He must not be hurt in any way.

All the same, her feet in the pretty satin evening slippers were not moving with their usual lightness when Diane made her way down to the main *sala*. The door was open and Alonso was already there in evening dress, the lights glancing on his crisp dark hair and deep tan in a way that never failed to quicken her pulse and bring the heat to her cheeks. The sea of carpet stretched between them and she walked across it gracefully, keeping her eyes lowered.

Alonso was in the act of pouring out wine from a crystal decanter on the sideboard, and he put it down immediately to greet her.

'How are you feeling?' he asked smoothly, his dark eyes enigmatic as he directed her to a chair. 'No more pains in the head, I trust? A little wine is called for to bring the colour back to those pale cheeks. Incidentally, the doctor assures me that the wound on your head will heal with scarcely a hint that it has been there.' He leaned over her to peer at the adhesive dressing now almost indiscernible among the red-gold curls, and Diane drew back from his masculine fragrance as if she had been stung. If he noticed the action he did not betray the fact but went on smoothly, 'The thought that there might be a scar has distressed you, no doubt?'

Diane quivered inwardly. There was something in the

air, a kind of electricity that was affecting her strangely. There was something different about him, something beneath that lazy nonchalant walk as he went across the room to fetch the two glasses of wine he had poured out, that could explode at the drop of a hat. The brief respite gave her time to collect herself. But her eyes rose no higher than the glass of wine he offered, and her hand carefully avoided contact with those strong fingers.

She said evenly, 'The thought did upset me a little until the doctor assured me that my fears were groundless.'

The room seemed to have assumed a listening quality as though waiting for the third guest. Dreading to know but unable to resist the demon of doubt already poised to strike a mortal blow at her shaky heart, Diane took the plunge.

'I thought Senhorita Vangroot would be here.'

Alonso did not answer at once but took a sip of his wine and waited for her to follow suit. Nervously she drank a little to give her the courage to hear what he had to say.

'Would you have been upset to see Bella here?' he asked slowly as he backed the fireplace.

'Why should I?' she answered, and wished he would sit down.

'I was hoping that there would be two reasons why you would resent her presence.' He put down his glass of wine as though he had lost the taste for it, turned slowly to face her and leaned indolently back against the fireplace. 'Shall we discuss the first reason? What were you doing at Bella's house? You must have been aware of the danger.'

Diane looked down into her wine. 'Senhora Vangroot asked me to go with her to pick up a few of her cherished possessions. She didn't want any fuss and I was the most likely one to ask. She told me that you had forbidden her to go to the *quinta* because it was unsafe.'

'Yet you went?' His voice thickened and he went on. rapidly. 'Do you not realise even now the—the miraculous escape you had from serious injury, even worse, when I . . .'

He broke off to clear his throat and Diane looked up at him in alarm. Her throat closed on the threat of swallowing

184

tears. He was thinking about Bella, of course. She might have been the one to sustain injuries, and the mere thought of it was making him draw a distracted hand across the dark hair. The thought occurred that he might be blaming her for Bella's visit to the *quinta*. Well, let him. What did it matter? It was only another thing to be blamed for.

'I—I'm sorry,' she faltered. 'I never meant to upset anyone.'

'You are sorry?' He glowered down at her. 'Why did you not leave a message here to say where you were going? You might have been trapped with no one knowing where you were.'

Diane moistened dry lips. 'But I thought Senhorita Vangroot had told you. How did you know I was there?'

He said grimly, 'Carlos sent me a message to say that he had taken two of you to Bella's *quinta* and had only collected one. I went immediately.'

She moved uneasily. 'Well, no harm has been done,' she said. 'I fell through the floor in the nursery, but the carpet cushioned my fall.'

Alonso stared at her in horror, said something explosive in Portuguese and thrust his hands into his pockets as if to keep them from violence.

'So,' he glared, 'you receive a wound on the head, innumerable bruises, and slight concussion, not to mention almost driving me mad, and no harm is done?'

Diane was noplussed. 'Well, Bella is all right, isn't she?'

He looked at her then as though she was out of her mind. 'Must you keep mentioning that woman?' he demanded. 'Have I not had more than enough of her for the past year? Why do you think I tolerated her for so long? I will tell you. She was on the brink of selling her estate to a speculator with plans to turn out the tenant farmers and convert the place into a huge holiday camp. I could not allow that to happen as the estates also bordered on mine. So I made her a generous offer and bided my time, hoping she would accept. I am no fool, and as time went on I realised that money was not the only price she required me to pay. Then

185

the fire seemed to precipitate matters, for Bella at least. When I brought her back here to the Quinta de Valmardi she finally decided to accept my offer. That was when Mother went with us to Funchal to sign the necessary papers. On our return Bella give me to understand that she regarded my giving her shelter at the Quinta as the equivalent to a proposal of marriage.' For the first time his face relaxed into the vestige of a smile. 'I had to tell her then that, as far as she was concerned, I had never had marriage in mind.'

Diane blinked, wondering if she had heard aright. 'You hadn't?' she gasped.

'No,' decisively, 'Definitely not. and now that we have dispensed with the first reason why Bella's presence would not please you, we will come to the second. Would my marriage to Bella have brought you distress?'

Diane stared down at her hands tightly clasped in her lap. In a low voice, she said, 'I felt that you wouldn't have been happy with her.'

'And my happiness is important to you?'

Diane bit hard on her lip, keeping her eyes lowered. If he did not guess already that she loved him he would soon know.

'Will you please leave me alone,' she cried. 'I don't feel well. I'm going to my room.'

Suddenly she was on her feet and making for the door. Then Alonso was behind her, gripping her upper arms and drawing her back against him.

'Diane, *pequena*,' he whispered in the side of her neck. 'Did you want a more exciting proposal? Shall I sweep you up in my arms and ride away with you as you watched Felipe do with Maria this afternoon?'

For blissful moments Diane had been bemused by the feel of his arms around her and his lips on her neck. Then as the import of what he was saying got through to her, she knew he was not only letting her know about Felipe and Maria, he was also taunting her.

Twisting from his grip, she faced him like a small fury.

'Isn't it enough for you to have gained your objective without getting at me? Yes, I did watch Felipe ride with Maria to his *quinta*. But I didn't do it for you. I did it for Maria, because I know that she truly loves Felipe. Now have the decency to let me go!'

He caught her hands, and when she struggled to free them, his grip tightened.

'I can never let you go, because you are a part of me,' he said heavily. 'I have wanted you from the moment I fell in love with your photograph. Later when I met you in Funchal for the first time, I wanted to carry you off like that ancestor of mine did and lock you up until you had promised to marry me. I wanted to forget Bella and her estate and declare my love for you there and then—but *pequena*, I had a duty towards those families on her estate. I had to try and save their homes, their jobs. So I had to be patient, I had to hurt you with words, and accusations that were not important, as an armour covering my love for you. When I carried you to my car from the ruins of her *quinta* that day I wanted to cover your unconscious little face with kisses. Later, I had to make my visits to your room very brief in case I betrayed my love for you. Everything had to be settled first with Bella.'

He was drawing her towards him and Diane was staring up into his face as though mesmerised. It could not be true, this feeling of her bones melting at his touch as his arms tightened around her. She felt his hard cheek pressing against her soft one and closed her eyes.

'You are my life. I love you with every beat of my heart. Tell me that you love me, that you will marry me as soon as possible.'

His lips were moving up the side of her neck, and poor Diane tried to keep a firm grip on her floating senses. 'But—Bella? Where is she?' she stammered. 'You—didn't say. I understood that there were to be three for dinner this evening.'

Alonso lifted his head and smiled down into her quivering face. 'Mother ordered dinner for three because she was

187

not to know about Maria going away with Felipe. As for Bella, she never returned here after taking you to her house that day. I neither know where she is, nor do I care. All I care about is you, *pequena*. We are going to be wonderfully happy. Now tell me that you love me.'

But whatever words Diane might have uttered were crushed against her lips by his demanding mouth. And as his kisses deepened in passion, she knew that the miracle of Alonso loving her was real. Later, there would be time to reveal in the joy of having Maria for a real sister. But not now, not while she was swooning with bliss in Alonso's arms. Her arms crept up slowly around his neck.

Did you miss any of these exciting Harlequin Omnibus 3-in-1 volumes?

Anne Hampson

Anne Hampson #3
Heaven Is High (#1570)
Gold Is the Sunrise (#1595)
There Came a Tyrant (#1622)

Essie Summers

Essie Summers #6
The House on Gregor's Brae (#1535)
South Island Stowaway (#1564)
A Touch of Magic (#1702)

Margaret Way

Margaret Way #2
Summer Magic (#1571)
Ring of Jade (#1603)
Noonfire (#1687)

Margaret Malcolm

Margaret Malcolm #2
Marriage by Agreement (#1635)
The Faithful Rebel (#1664)
Sunshine on the Mountains (#1699)

Eleanor Farnes

Eleanor Farnes #2
A Castle in Spain (#1584)
The Valley of the Eagles (#1639)
A Serpent in Eden (#1662)

Kay Thorpe

Kay Thorpe
Curtain Call (#1504)
Sawdust Season (#1583)
Olive Island (#1661)

18 magnificent Omnibus volumes to choose from:

Betty Neels

Betty Neels #3
Tangled Autumn (#1569)
Wish with the Candles (#1593)
Victory for Victoria (#1625)

Violet Winspear

Violet Winspear #5
Raintree Valley (#1555)
Black Douglas (#1580)
The Pagan Island (#1616)

Anne Hampson

Anne Hampson #4
Isle of the Rainbows (#1646)
The Rebel Bride (#1672)
The Plantation Boss (#1678)

Margery Hilton

Margery Hilton
The Whispering Grove (#1501)
Dear Conquistador (#1610)
Frail Sanctuary (#1670)

Rachel Lindsay

Rachel Lindsay
Love and Lucy Granger (#1614)
Moonlight and Magic (#1648)
A Question of Marriage (#1667)

Jane Arbor

Jane Arbor #2
The Feathered Shaft (#1443)
Wildfire Quest (#1582)
The Flower on the Rock (#1665)

Great value in reading at $2.25 per volume

Joyce Dingwell

Joyce Dingwell #3
Red Ginger Blossom (#1633)
Wife to Sim (#1657)
The Pool of Pink Lilies (#1688)

Hilary Wilde

Hilary Wilde
The Golden Maze (#1624)
The Fire of Life (#1642)
The Impossible Dream (#1685)

Flora Kidd

Flora Kidd
If Love Be Love (#1640)
The Cave of the White Rose (#1663)
The Taming of Lisa (#1684)

Lucy Gillen

Lucy Gillen #2
Sweet Kate (#1649)
A Time Remembered (#1669)
Dangerous Stranger (#1683)

Gloria Bevan

Gloria Bevan
Beyond the Ranges (#1459)
Vineyard in a Valley (#1608)
The Frost and the Fire (#1682)

Jane Donnelly

Jane Donnelly
The Mill in the Meadow (#1592)
A Stranger Came (#1660)
The Long Shadow (#1681)

Complete and mail this coupon today!